CASAROJA

a novel by

Michael Morow

WingSpan Press

Copyright © 2014 by Michael Morow

All rights reserved.

This book is a work of fiction. Names, characters, settings and incidents are either the product of the author's imagination or used fictitiously. Any resemblance to actual events, settings or persons, living or dead, is entirely coincidental.

No part of this book may be reproduced or transmitted in any form or by any means, electronic or mechanical, including photocopying, recording or by any information storage and retrieval system, without written permission from the author, except for the inclusion of brief quotations in reviews.

Published in the United States and the United Kingdom
by WingSpan Press, Livermore, CA

The WingSpan name, logo and colophon are the trademarks of WingSpan Publishing.

ISBN 978-1-59594-526-6 (pbk.)
ISBN 978-1-59594-683-6 (hardcover)

First edition 2014

Printed in the United States of America

www.wingspanpress.com

Library of Congress Control Number 2014938533

1 2 3 4 5 6 7 8 9 10

constituting book 6 of the cycle in progress

THE LONG EXILE

The versions of Psalms 136 and 42 are from The Holy Bible: Douay Rheims Version, Revised by Bishop Richard Challoner a.d. 1749-1752 (John Murphy Company, Baltimore 1899).

The quotation of Benedict's rule regarding the abbot is from The Rule of Saint Benedict, translated with an introduction by Cardinal Gasquet (Chatto & Windus, London 1925).

Contents

The Journey 1

June 1988 37

The Dance of the Conquistadors 55

Casaroja 80

The Day in the Sun 94

The Day of Shadows 128

Requiem 153

Departings 159

Gifts 172

A Note on the Author *177*

A Note on Design .... *179* for Jewell with love

Everyman: Farewell, good Fellowship! For this my heart is sore;
Adieu forever! I shall see thee no more.

Fellowship: In faith, Everyman, farewell now at the ending;
For you I will remember that parting is mourning.

Everyman (ca. 1485).

THE JOURNEY

At last light they heard a figure on horseback approaching the crest of the hill. There was a rustling of big leaves and the fluttering snort of the horse, obviously tired from the effort. Then followed what seemed the murmur of a rider's voice, reassuring the horse. From their vantage point, half-hidden by thick pine branches along the side of the rough path, the two men watched in complete silence. The rider had stopped, it seemed, to rest the horse. Or perhaps he, in turn, was peering into the dense wall of trees in search of them. It did not seem they had made any noise.

The man known as Felipe crouched lower under the branches and quietly scooted forward for a better view. His companion sat immobile, holding his knees and staring forward like a tiny figurine. This man Toda, a Kekchi Mayan, was along for his knowledge of the terrain and his ability to speak to the people they would encounter on this journey. He had nothing to do at present and, besides, was justifiably wary. Felipe whispered to Toda to stay put; he was safely invisible especially at this hour of twilight. Toda appeared to remain in that position of fixed immobility as Felipe turned away from him and inched ahead. But the *indígena*'s right hand had found the blunt end of the dagger at his side, and he gripped it determinedly.

Felipe edged up to where a broad slice of the darkening valley lay before him. There was a very slight breeze, just enough to mask sound from this distance, but he realized how it also undercut his own security. On his knees and hands he searched the matrix of branches where the mounted figure had just briefly appeared. There was nothing to be seen. It was already noticeably darker; things could very quickly slip out of control...things could already be beyond control. Felipe did not have to place a muddied hand to his chest to know his heart was racing. *Where was the intruder now?* A sense of overwhelming dread suddenly engulfed him as he grasped the full life and death implications of that question. He was quick on his feet and cagey, but not made for this level of adventure, he suddenly realized. And he carried no weapon. Nor had he any inkling that his secretive companion, that stone-faced *indígena*, had one.

He looked up, craning his neck around, and was instantly blinded. A great dark form, looming right above him, had moved slightly back, allowing the dying crimson sunlight to flood Felipe's eyes. Back—a tree root blocked his progress. Left—he found himself staring at a horse's leg and a black boot, felt his whole mind explode forward as if pierced—

"Buenas tardes, señor."

The voice of the horseman was gruff, alien. Felipe steadied himself, managed to come to a half-standing crouch and looked up. A long silence, nothing else, just another and now very cool gust of breeze up from the valley across his face. *Or is that what it is?* He reached for his forehead, reacting tardily to what now seemed a splitting pain in his head. Stars already starting to appear around the edge of the silhouetted hat of the rider...*that fast?* Are such my last thoughts, Felipe cursed himself, neither a cry for help nor even a prayer? Then he heard the horse's fluttering again—long, rolling, fully relaxed. The animal was perfectly calm, Felipe's rational mind finally spoke to him. And another cool gust across his face startled him into the realization that the blinding light behind his eyes was not the result of a sudden blow to his head, nor a wound of any kind, but was only caused by terror: terror absolute. He was whole, he had not been attacked at all, though terrifying questions still danced along the knife edge of his surprised consciousness, all at once.

A soldier? The most vital question. But no...an *alien* voice, not from this country...and an ordinary boot and hat too. He quickly stole a glance at the intruder's collar...nothing unusual. Felipe leaned backward, still clumsy, plopped involuntarily into a sitting position, his awkwardness exposing his helplessness more than anything else could say. Nothing happened.

"Bueno." Felipe felt the voice just coming out of himself, as if from nowhere, replying to the stranger in *español* as he had been instructed...for reasons of which he had not been fully informed. "Ah, buenas noches, señor." He knew he was fighting to convey a bit of control both to himself and to the stranger, despite his awkwardness and blunders, and he hoped he had carried it off.

It seemed that the stranger nodded, very slightly, in acknowledgment.

Felipe could see now that this man was, in his own barely perceptible way, being very cagey too. He had bridled the horse slightly backwards so that now horse and rider were stamped before him in full relief. This was a very large framed man. He might well be the *americáno*, the priest that his friends had instructed him to meet near this point. But this fellow was a day ahead of schedule and loomed much bigger than the old photograph that Felipe had seen would have suggested. In any event Felipe found himself sitting entirely on the clearing of the path, exposed at least for the moment. Nothing bad had happened but the man had said nothing more, either. Felipe realized that he ought to be able to scamper away into the darkness quickly, if necessary. But the fellow had not made any move and it did not seem as if anyone else was following him.

The long pregnant silence expanded as, behind the stranger's black silhouette, the last long sliver of turquoise sky faded quickly away. Felipe had seen that the man's profile, under the hat, was mostly hidden by a *pañuelo* pulled up over his lower face. He felt himself shuddering, perhaps for the cooling air rustling the sweat which had broken out all over his exposed skin. But no, that was not the only reason. Felipe shuddered again. For while he did not know in detail the reasons for this mission, the man he was supposed to meet here tomorrow was certainly not supposed to be any sort of a *bandolero*.

"¿Hay un sendero a Casaroja, por favor?"

"Sí."

The words had shot suddenly from the figure, and Felipe's reply had been practically involuntary. But it had been a confirmation of sorts, and Felipe was deeply grateful. However incongruously, this reference seemed to indicate that this was the fellow he and Toda were here to watch for, and to accompany from this point onward.

"Iremos con él." Felipe stated clearly, back in the direction of Toda. There was no response.

"Elc chic us," Felipe stated now in Kekchi, imperatively. Then softened it, "K'aplisinc."

There was a rustling in the underbrush as Toda scooted out, somehow, while maintaining his same sitting position. It was very dark already but you could see his small white eyes, gleaming. He said nothing.

The horse whinnied fully for once, shuddering, entirely relaxing. The stranger neither said anything more nor removed his *pañuelo*. But as Felipe gained his night vision he seemed to notice that the fellow had a beard covering most of his face anyway, and long scraggly hair behind. He had no resemblance to the young, clean-cut *americáno* in that snapshot whatsoever. But if the figure said nothing more, he asked nothing more, either. Felipe remained sitting on his heels, with Toda slightly behind curled up in his characteristic posture.

"*Gracias*," the man eventually said lowly, gruffly, in the same indifferent tone that he used when he petted his mount. No, he clearly was not a *ladino* like himself, and certainly not an *indígena*, either. He was a *gringo* of some sort, alright, therefore not a soldier. If a revolutionary, a remote but nonetheless dangerous possibility not yet entirely to be dismissed, he quite obviously had come alone.

They would have to get moving. There was a little ways still to go for the night, Felipe eventually announced as flatly as he could manage it. This spot was not the best place to stay for the night; Toda had their burros safely hidden a little ways off.

"*Preferiría un campamento cerca de aquí*," the voice from the dark shape stated, just as flatly. He did not say why.

Felipe saw immediately it was useless to argue with this person, but his gesture or shudder must have conveyed the question.

"*Seguridad*."

That was all. Whether for his own safety or for all of theirs, the sphinxlike stranger would not say. Perhaps if he thought there was trouble a hilltop offered various strategic advantages, but it was not a decision Felipe would have made. The man's tone was oddly reassuring, though, and Felipe had cause to reflect that the more he heard this man speak, he *must* be the *americáno padre*, or some other *americáno*. The odd thing however was that this big *gringo* seemed just as at home, perhaps even more at home with the country than Felipe himself. Somehow, yes, Felipe was sure of it: *this man knows this place, this man has been here before*. But you could well dread that thought, too. Truth be told, Felipe did not like this business very much at all, but it was his *compañeros'* business and certainly they were all trustworthy…certainly…. Yet if the rider were that familiar with this terrain, Felipe wondered, why am I necessary at all?

No. He could not allow himself to think in that direction….

"Como usted quiera," Felipe said resignedly, but pronouncing it slowly, exactly, and as formally as he was capable.

"Estoy muy contento."

Is this *bandido* laughing at me, Felipe almost cried to himself? Felipe's *compadres* in Guatemala City seemed very far away right now, as far away as all the world.

A slim crescent moon began to emerge just above the pine tops. Felipe could see the figure backing away a little, staying out of sight. He apparently meant to camp by himself on the far side of the path. Felipe found himself standing up, finally.

"¿Cuál es…su…nombre de pila?" he forced himself to say to the retreating specter, as imperatively as he could without sacrificing the formality.

The shape of the mounted rider just stood there.

"Señor Cacique," the voice came directly, with great inflection.

Felipe felt the chill again, all over. Yes what an awful mess. There had been ice in that voice, and a rather snarling facetiousness, answered as if it were all part of a charade. This murderous *bandido* has smoked me out! And they sent me into this spot with this desperate alien, who knows this God-forsaken hilltop better than I do myself! Dear Mother of God!

But Felipe could see the man's hand raised now, a sort of salute, as he disappeared the short distance away toward the point from which he had first materialized. And Felipe believed he saw, at the last possible moment, that fellow's eyes and face, beneath all that hair and the *pañuelo*, crinkle into a smile.

*   *   *

The three made their way along the edge of the *altiplano*, on a narrow path shaded by tall trees. There was a constant wind today, sparing them from insects. Toda came up first on his burro, followed at some distance by Felipe on his. The stranger who called himself Señor Cacique, still shielding his face with that *pañuelo*, came up a few lengths at the rear, high up on his fine brown horse. From there it looked like he could see everything. He had had very little to say since breakfast and still made Felipe nervous, for it still could not be clear that he was the proper *americáno* and not a fraudulent impostor. The horse was impressive, well bred, not the sort of animal he had ever seen any poor missionary astride.

They were at least sixty *leguas* away from Casaroja, three long days' journey at least, perhaps more, especially given the *barranca* and the rough country ahead. For it was very fine with the wide, lime green valleys below to either side of the ridge they traversed, and you were tempted to forget about your worries although the question would only be more troubling as they approached their particular destination. This might be a very bad fellow for sure, and this whole adventure the greatest of follies. Felipe, when he allowed himself to think about it, cursed himself angrily for his great gullibility, into being tricked into such a scheme.

And what was it for? Certainly not for any remuneration at all, however it might well end in his own death or the death of others. ¡Bobo! ¡Idiota! ¡Simploanzo! What a way to end your life, with a big blood-thirsty *americáno vaquero*—oh, *malo, malo!* He is a bad one, I am sure! Felipe had seen many American Westerns in his home of recent years in Guatemala City, near the *universidad*—especially including the very latest epics starring Clint Eastwood. He could remember plainly those villains sitting around waiting at the train station, their big ugly faces filling the screen as flies buzzed about them. Oh Santa María, dear Mother of God, this one is precisely like them, I am sure, when he pulls that devilish *pañuelo* down! Señor Cacique is in with the revolutionaries, I know it! And I am leading him to Casaroja! Even worse things than all that has happened are going to come down on our heads, and I am the cause of it!

But oh, he will never take that mask off, either. What a sly one!

Felipe had inched over at the crack of dawn, carefully, with a cup full of *posal* for breakfast. He had fallen asleep the night before feeling good about the fellow, the way his eyes had seemed to smile. But how wrong he had been, he was now sure. The big gruff beast had seemed to sense his approach, turned over on his poncho. *Fíjate*, Felipe had cried to himself, look! He still wore his *pañuelo*, even in his sleep! And he was stirring awake—

"¡Aléjate! ¡Quítate de delante!"

Felipe had fallen back a little at these commands, too stunned to realize that he was still holding out the little cup of breakfast to the monster, like an offering.

"¡Quitádmelo de delante!" the stranger roared, "¡Basta, no más!"

Felipe's hair bristled as he retreated, cold sweat again. Oh, what was the fellow reaching at his side for? Felipe did not even look; he turned curtly and marched away.

"Como usted quiera," Felipe announced in as plain and unruffled a tone as he could muster, without any note of deference or respect. As you wish! He gathered up all of his bravery to walk away, too, his back to Señor Cacique. Yes, shoot me now, coward! Then he thought better of it—practically scampered away for the safety of the trees!

After a while more nasty commands followed across the way. Faster! Out of here by the light!

And so the day had begun. And what a beautiful day, too! Big blue black headed jays flapped loudly just over their heads, not shy at all, crossing from one side of the steep ridgeline to the other. In the far distance blue mountains shone under the sun, their peaks and mounds etched clearly against the sky. And, as the day's light became fuller, the subtle hues of fir, pine, and juniper enveloped them; fresh scents filled their nostrils as they progressed along the *altiplano* trail. What a paradise this was, Felipe remembered, not having been along this precise way for several years. What a paradise and what a hell—to be in this place, with that diabolical giant following behind! Felipe had half-turned toward him once, to assure himself Señor Cacique was still there, but also as a sort of peace offering. The growling had begun almost at once! What a life, and what a way for it to end! That sullen peasant Toda had the right idea though—keeping the

Casaroja

length of a good soccer field ahead. Ready to disappear quickly at the first gunshot—also well too advanced along the trail for a cold blade in the back!

At midday they reached a broad saddle where three hills joined. Toda stopped and Felipe caught up with him. Dismounting, they crouched in the shade and mixed bowls of *posal*. Seeing them thus engaged, the spook backed off and took his own meal break alone. They watched him warily as a sheet of mist drifted in close overhead, laden with rain. The downpour just missed them and they could hear it roaring down just over the crest to the east, lightning bolts flashing ahead of it further downslope.

As they were finishing they watched the *americáno* slowly approach them up the path, big heavy steps. A sack dangled over his shoulder, from which he shortly produced a handful of crisp *totopostes*. The giant crouched down right before them, handed a few across for them to sample.

Toda just glared, his muscles tightening and flexing, his eyes shining white in a look that would be interpreted anywhere on earth as malice absolute, as if trapped. Yet full of menace and threat, to his last breath if pushed that far. Then the native summarily stood and walked straightway up the road, taking the leash of his burro and leading it away.

Felipe was only perplexed, tired already of the stranger's mercurial mood shifts, the way he waxed and waned. Obviously this was Señor Cacique's own sort of peace offering. Felipe would have shuddered again if there was a shudder left in him, but he found himself hardening somewhat into a self-protective aloofness. Oh well, humor the oaf, Felipe's survival instinct told him. You may learn something useful but be careful not to let your guard down.

"Gracias. Bueno," Felipe heard himself saying as he carefully slid one and only one piece from Señor Cacique's open hand. He crunched it and washed it down his throat, a long gulp from his flask. Oh my, and that was a sweet one, too! His arm automatically snapped out, his hand snatching two more.

Saying nothing, Señor Cacique seemed to nod a little, as if acknowledging him. Then Felipe wearily watched the *americáno* sauntering away. Bastard! Felipe heard his inner voice cursing himself again, you baboon! This murderer is so easily putting you into the palm of his hand! Resist him and stay alert, for your good life's sake, Felipe!

But then, as the stranger was gone away from him, Felipe mused otherwise. Yes, I did get something sound back from him, after all, something I dearly need: I got a good look at him, at last. And what a fright!

This was certainly not the person Felipe's *compañeros* had told him about, no, not either in character or aspect. The men of the brotherhood would never esteem such a one. He lurched about, all six feet of his hulking frame, and came up to you practically bandy-legged. You could not say that he was an obese fatso, yet too he quite obviously relished his food. You could hear him back there smacking his lips, crunching up *totopostes* at practically a gulp, clearly a total *rústico*. No emaciated *penitente* this! There was also of course that horrible blue *pañuelo* that seemed permanently glued to his face, and a big ugly black *sombrero*, precisely of the sort evil *americáno* cowboys wore. And finally there was the give-away: that fantastic oversized belt buckle, pure silver, to hold in his gut. A fine piece of loot for a man of his purported calling! *¡Válgame Dios!* And what was depicted upon this monstrosity—Our Lady of Guadalupe, a good saint, the face of our suffering Lord? *¡Nada de eso!* A flying snake sticking out its forked tongue, embossed against what looked like a perversity of the striped *americáno* flag! There was some sort of magic oath in *inglés* etched beneath it, shouting out at you with an exclamation point—¡Madre María! It was no wonder the monster smelled so—as if he had been out in the country not for mere days, but for years, and never bathing. Hell was this one's home, for sure. Oh how had the brotherhood's plans become known to this impostor, and what had he done to that heroic young *padre* in the photo?

Well, at least they were back on the path, and Señor Cacique was apparently so satiated with food that his endless, insulting commands had stopped. But how am I going to get out of this, Felipe wondered. And an even darker thought, that he had dared not broach but which he could no longer allow himself the luxury to avoid: what if the brotherhood has been penetrated? Who was the Judas? It was certainly not unknown in recent years that such things could occur. Certainly not Ignacio. Not Lupe. There was that new man, who called himself Juan de la Cruz. Please, Lord. Felipe could not bear to think of it. I have to get back to warn them! Maybe they will all be in trouble already! But how am I going to get away from this malicious oaf, to carry it off?

On a broad shelf between peaks they were going through a ruin of an old plantation now, one of those that used to be owned by Germans before the Second World War, whose lands had been confiscated. It was above a southwestern facing slope, and they were all in the open sun. There were some signs of habitation more recently, but no one around. The dirt road widened and flattened, along some poorly maintained fence lines overgrown with lush pink-flowered vines. There came that sound of a high, then low double note *wheech-oo, wheech-oo*, rising as it was repeated; a beautiful quetzal, curling its tail, sang from a sad, droopy tree just ahead. Felipe looked up as they passed under it, seeing its deep indigo blue and purple feathers. The he closed his eyes, took in a deep breath out of the air rich with the smell of a world in bloom—ah, the delicious scent of freedom! I could get away now, Felipe mused, just run! But the *americáno* coming up behind made him uneasy, and in truth he did not wholly trust that inscrutable Toda either, far in front. Better wait until nightfall.

Felipe heard an odd sound behind. He stopped and turned, and was confronted by the preposterous sight of Señor Cacique reaching his great bear-like arms into the banana trees growing abundantly here, picking off a cluster of bananas, and then ripping their skins off. Felipe then heard sort of a growl, quickly turned back around. Shortly he heard the beast consuming the bananas in big gulps. It was more than he could bear! And you could hear him licking his chops across the whole countryside!

But the landscape turned again, as switchbacks criss-crossed upslope to a steep crest. They were back into wilderness and the old mountain pass. Toda had practically disappeared ahead and Felipe could not make him out until he was well along on this path himself, again. The afternoon was lengthening; new grey clouds were menacing, closer and lower. A very cold wind hit them now, refreshing and colder than anything he had felt for days. But it obviously portended a great storm and very soon.

Felipe looked left and right. Ridges fell off dramatically to each side here—nowhere to go. The path seemed to rise even more steeply ahead and he watched the shape of Toda on his burro climb and then disappear over that next peak. On his way up a sheet of rain hit him full in the face, ice cold and drenching.

Then immediately over the crest the landscape plunged.

Down, down.... Felipe was thinking of his animal's footing in the already dangerous mud between rocks, and of where the narrow path was. He was trying to be very careful to stay on that path and not lose Toda. The *bobo!* Why did he get so far ahead? He was thinking of all these things and of how the lightning cracked and resounded in the dense green forest closing in on him, when he finally remembered that yes, this was where the first great *barranca* began, the steep rocky ravines dropping ultimately into the western valley. All was invisible behind the close verdant vegetation and the rain. That last crest had been the end of the *altiplano* trail and now he was trapped.

The *americáno's* horse snorted roughly, right behind him, pushing its nose right into his own burro. He turned and saw the mad look on that animal's face, barely held in control by the figure under the drenched black *sombrero*, his white eyes gleaming above that hateful blue *pañuelo*. Too late! There was nothing to be done but to hold on for dear life down this treacherous gorge, trapped on a steep descent into this green hell with a demon breathing down his back.

*   *   *

Then came another day of rain, and another. They had gone down into two canyons along their descent and then up again, miraculously without serious injury or losing an animal. Now they were slowly descending yet another rocky gorge. The weather had significantly slowed their progress, by at least a full day. They were drenched and covered with mud, and their clothes had torn with their falls. They all had cuts and scrapes on knees and elbows from falling on slippery rock, and all had helped each other up more than once out of the dark brown muck. The paths were so rough and impossible, the ground so treacherously loose and thick, that much of the time they were simply walking the animals.

It was mid-morning of still another day of this weather with no end in sight. They had just started down into this next great gorge when lightning ripped out of the sky all around, very close to them and as terrifying as Felipe had ever remembered. Just ahead it had hit the hillside, everything going blinding white all around them like a great explosion. Wondrously though, a small cave opened up alongside of the trail. It had just enough room for the three of them. So there they sat, handing *posal* and *totopostes* around. And silent as three deaf mutes, with the vast hollow sounds of the storm enveloping the world beyond. The flashes of lightning made everything very strange and eerie, and it was even stranger to observe the beast—his *pañuelo* pulled up over his entire nose just under his eyelids, casually feeding himself beneath it. He was sticking the crusty bread up inside that blue mask, spooning the *posal* in there.

This silence was the way the tensions among them had finally been resolved. In truth, Felipe reflected, no one had said hardly a word for two days. One would think that the terrible situation they shared would have brought them closer together, but that was far from the case. They were closer only in the sense of their physical proximity. In every other way things had remained the same, and in many ways they were further apart than ever. Since they had begun this trek cutting across the highlands, gradually down, the strange *americáno* had taken to camping so far away from the others at night that they could not have found him if they had to. They had to wait for him to show up each morning to get going.

Toda, at least, had ceased staring daggers at the fellow. But the *indígena* just looked straight ahead blankly like an everyday lunatic, entirely detached within his own universe. As for Señor Cacique, he was wary as ever and he seemed to have figured out that he was being watched closely and that he was entirely distrusted. He accepted that without rancor, it seemed, and had also ceased all his little commands—there was no place for them now, anyway.

Felipe had felt that terrible urge to warm up to the *gringo* again, especially when they had begun sharing real hardships. The first time the giant had stooped down to throw him a helping hand had been a great relief—it really helped him too as he had come down in a particularly bad spot, wedged between slick boulders. Also, with real troubles on their hands, Felipe started thinking of what a total irrational fool he himself was becoming, the prisoner of all sorts of absurd and illusory fears. What has gotten into me? The *compañeros* had asked me if I was up to this daring venture, and I said yes. Obviously they put great trust in me, he thought, and I cannot spoil everything with this womanish fear.

But then had come something which Felipe did not dream up, he knew. Although it was so entirely unexpected, unambiguous, and terrifying that it made him question his very sanity. At the crest of a flat hillside between gullies yesterday afternoon, the rain had stopped for a time. They were sitting around resting for a meal. Señor Cacique as usual had disappeared, and Felipe had not even been looking for him. Felipe had just been walking around, to relieve his aching legs, when he thought he heard a voice, sharply through the thick jungle. He carefully approached that sound and saw, some distance off, the *americáno* walking around delivering some sort of directions or commands, as it were, to the trees. Perhaps Señor Cacique thought he was Saint Francis or perhaps he was cracking up, who knows. Felipe drew as close as he dared.

He then plainly perceived a little telephone or radio of some sort in the *americáno's* hand, which the fellow was so insistently barking into. He was speaking in a combination of *inglés* and Spanish, mostly *inglés*. Felipe could make very little of it out at all, except that the words very clearly included commands and references to geography. And then one terribly clear directive rang out through the woods, dire and monstrous:

"Él ha retirado sus fordos. ¡Entrégale al Hermano Cochino el último golpe! ¿De qué se sirve esperar más? *La Sangre de cerdo fresco es el vino de los ángeles.*"

Those last unforgettable words, obviously a death sentence, were delivered with a devilish curling snarl as the Yankee bit off the end of the sentence, clearly relishing the sadistic butchery to follow.

Dear Lord in Heaven!

Felipe crossed himself as he backed out of sight of the monster as quietly yet quickly as was possible. Pigs to the slaughterhouse! He was so horrified at what he had heard that, only some distance away, did he realize for the first time he had seen the face of the impostor without that horrid *pañuelo*. Oh, how awful beyond words! *¡Qué monstruo horrible!* A thick curling moustache covering his whole mouth, his whole face covered with hair like an ape man!

And Felipe knew terribly, immediately, that there was only one thing to be done. He instinctively banished the thought but it did not depart. The thought was in no hurry to leave now that it had come. It would wait its own time and it was plain, apparent. Oh yes, Felipe would find himself saying it to himself again, closing his eyes but suddenly unable to pray anymore. Yes. No other choice: I must somehow kill this impostor.

How in the world, though, could that be done? The man was big and tough looking. And so alert, constantly on the watch. At night Señor Cacique was in hiding; there seemed no way to surprise him. Yet Felipe could conceive of no other course. If the man was not stopped, horror was sure to follow. He was in with those security parties, Felipe now was sure, the army. Or perhaps with the revolutionaries. Either way, what difference did it make? Both were to blame for all the death which had swept this land, the destruction of entire villages. It is coming to Casaroja, and I am bringing it! This thought filled all Felipe's mind, the moment he thought about anything other than his own safety at this moment. He felt himself swinging from one overwhelming panic to the next, suddenly holding on with all his might to retain his sanity. I must maintain some clarity, he desperately thought, but I must also act quickly before both we two and that village are all obliterated! "*Sangre de cerdo fresco....*" Dear, dear God!

Once during that last, long cold night, it had occurred to Felipe that he had never even thought, once in his life, of any kind of killing. Then he would shudder and shrink from it...no, it was like murder, was it not? Then no, no, definitely: it was not. It was the protection of all those others. It was necessary, it was even noble—for it would be cowardly to shrink from it and to fail. It was even a duty....

But was some alternative possible? Perhaps we could just sneak away and leave Señor Cacique lost.... Perhaps I could only wound him...but how even to do that?

Two nights ago he had finally seen Toda's dagger, its hilt catching a gleam of moonlight that also caught the sullen *indígena*'s eyes. Ha! Felipe had thought then, good for you! In one way it had merely confirmed what he had believed all along about this hard-bitten fellow: looking out for himself first and foremost. But Felipe had been heartened too, to know that he had a companion with both such foresight and grim determination. I should have had more of both!

Now he had to gently but firmly coax that weapon into his own hands, for his own deadly business. He knew a little Kekchi; he was sure that this, even more than his familiarity with the terrain, was why the brotherhood had chosen him for this mission. Indeed, he saw with terrible clarity, it was providential: it was for precisely this moment.

So last night he had waited until the *americáno* was safely away. Then waited some more, and crawled over to where Toda crouched for some shelter under the broad leaves of a giant fern. They were almost to the bottom of this canyon but it was a broad one, and somewhat open at the point they had come to stop this night. The storms seemed to be receding. The moon, a bright waxing crescent, cracked through the cloud cover close to midnight, illuminating their surroundings to a degree unsurpassed for many days. The *indígena* was getting a little sloppy; his dagger's handle was even more plain to see than it had been before. Nonetheless Felipe had so far refrained from calling attention to it, or from giving any suggestion that he knew about it. No telling what reaction that would bring. That moment would await its right time. For now, he just lightly touched the dozing native's sleeve, as not to startle him.

Toda wakened; his eyes blinked. He startled as he saw Felipe's form right before him. Felipe already had his finger to his lips—a sign of *silencio*.

"Ch'anch'o" Felipe whispered, "U*ybenc*."

Toda understood. Felipe could see the Indian's nostrils flare slightly, his eyes narrow. He was already fully awake and acutely aware of the situation. He understood perfectly. His eyes blinked again, the long lashes curling almost as if they too were straining to sense the unspoken threat in the night.

Of course, too, Toda's right hand already instinctively grasped the blade handle. That could wait, as for the first time Felipe unabashedly shared with the Kekchi that sense of imminent threat and danger which seemed the *indígena*'s constant companion.

A bird's cry, distant but shrill, broke the silence regularly. There was a light wind, occasionally rustling the leaves, and from time to time it also brought the sounds of nocturnal animals, growling and sputtering. But there were no other sounds. Now and then the leaves above them would drip; the atmosphere all around was charged with rich smells of the vegetation and the earth, but there was nothing unusual apparent, nothing seeming to move toward them. Señor Cacique was obviously far away, so far they could not hear him snoring, not even hear his horse. So much the better. After some minutes Toda seemed to subtly change expression, take on an inquisitive gleam as his face hardened behind roiling eyes.

This was the moment Felipe had been waiting for. As Toda's face started to fully turn, his lips parting, showing his amazingly intact set of white teeth, Felipe was set. He met Toda's question fully, bringing down his right forefinger to point quickly and directly at the blade handle, mere inches away—

"*Šh*camic," Felipe whispered intently in the hush, his lips smacking as he practically spit out the Kekchi consonants. And said to himself resolutely: "Yes: *su muerte:* his death."

And yes, too: he could see immediately that the native agreed, even as his body shifted away, holding the weapon farther out of Felipe's reach. His teeth were gritting, his lips curling into a mask of ultimate disdain.

Felipe pointed at the weapon directly again, but unthreateningly, emphasizing that he wished it to be handed over freely. "K'anjorinc," he gestured, one hand open, the other brushing back toward his breast. "Usilal lain," his whisper was almost pleading, humble—oh grant me this favor, Toda!

"Uggh!" The tough little man grunted, in universal language, "Ecchh!"

There was fear in Toda's eyes. Simply, he conveyed to Felipe his belief that the *ladino* could not get the job done. Or perhaps it was just a complication of an enterprise already fatally flawed from this fatalistic little man's perspective. In any event, Felipe had to think fast. He would never regain Toda's trust if he failed now; the native, with his needed weapon, would stay far away from him from here on. Things were always, with these people, simple beyond simplicity. And it would certainly not do to admit, one iota, the cagey Indian's perception of his own questionable courage....

"*Tento!*" Felipe suddenly growled back at Toda, daring to rise above the whispering. And just pushed his hand out in a demanding fashion—and spit it out, fiercely in Spanish—"¡Dámelo!" Yes, give it to me now, slave—"¡Pronto!"

The lock opened instantly, of that awful safe burned upon the soul of the *indígena*. The knife was produced and laid flat out straight in Felipe's hand. Toda again sat motionless, expressionless, bolt upright in his ordinary pose of vast inscrutability. Yes, Felipe thought, with a tinge of awful sickness that was not completely banished by his triumph, the great majority of them will still open to that combination. Although the revolution had undone the code in many, left it forever scrambled. It disgusted Felipe, with himself, that he had to call up that wretched curse of their country's history. But there had been no other choice. Sweet Jesu, it was almost as if one could hear the tumblers clicking....

It had been a gamble, too. On the Indian and his soundness. The brotherhood vouched for him but they could have been hoodwinked. There had been no way of telling what in the world was going on in this country for years. And up to now, come to think of it, there had been little enough communication of any kind between Felipe and the native, much less anything this deep. And that is my fault, Felipe accused himself ruefully, I have been careless about asserting my command. Toda was quite right to sneer at my weakness.

But on another level, no, Felipe thought. I must mend this quickly, and make him understand that I use him not merely as a tool. Fine, he said to himself, but I am just not up to that part. Help me, dear Mother of God, help me make him see. We are not to treat one such as him as a slave; he deserves an explanation.

"Toda," Felipe quietly addressed him familiarly, "Bueno."

The fellow did not flinch.

"K'un šól." Felipe pronounced it slowly, patting his own heart with his fist.

Toda sort of snorted, but involuntarily. Anyway, he had acknowledged. Sorry, friend, Felipe thought, but this is how I am. Now drive the point home.

"Tento," he said, if softly now. And then explained, "No *presbítero*, no *padre*. No, no, no." He was quite sure that Toda understood that much Spanish, but he repeated it for him in his own language—"Inc' a yucua'."

"Eeech!" Almost a laugh. As if anyone could be so *estúpido* to have ever believed that—another response bordering on rebuke. The native's teeth gleamed in silent mockery.

Enough of this, Felipe thought, you *garañón*. Managing not to snarl back, Felipe curtly dismissed him. Toda got up, walked slowly away without making a sound.

Felipe tucked the knife away safely at his side, fashioning a sheath out of the pouch for his water bottle.

No—I cannot do it right now, he thought, I have to think. And how to find the beast in this night?

Felipe was thinking of all the problems he had, intermittently trying to pray for strength. He watched another charcoal cloud cross the moon, right above and very bright again. The sheer weight of all these problems...how...how.... And under all those conflicting pressures he quickly and involuntarily found a way out of all of it. In sleep....

*   *   *

I must kill Señor Cacique....

A voice, his own it seemed, but new and strange jolted him up deeply out of himself. He found himself sitting in a pool of moonlight with an unsheathed dagger in his right hand, his arms out at the ready....

How did I get here? Well that was very plain...Inés, oh Inés.... He saw her before her parent's *chabola*, so good to see her again. He had been running up the road toward her, he remembered, and it seemed endless: rows of tall trees to either side, streaming in the wind, dogs running quickly by and past him in the opposite direction, clouds passing overhead, the sky changing colors...then night and moon, then day and sun. Is that a boy I see in your arms, is that our little *hijo espúreo*? "Oh!" he cried through his sweat as he ran, his eyes closing in remorse, "Anything, anything...as you say, dearest Inés, I will never leave you again, never, I will...."

But as he reached the end of his sprint a great flame stood before him, dead center against the humble little *casa*: Inés in flames...Inés *a* flame...a tongue of bright red enveloping her but yet she stood, immobile, her long black dress glowing, her eyes shining and her black hair flying in the wind as she held out to him not a child but a dagger, a piercing blue glint straight out to her side, outside of her cocoon of fire, shining so bright it hurt his eyes....

He felt his heart pounding as the dirt sped away beneath his feet, yet she seemed to draw only slowly closer.... He narrowed his gaze, tried to fix his eyes on that blue-white blaze. He felt his feet pounding the earth beneath him, heard the sound they made... harder...*harder*....

"Dios te salve María, llena eres de gracia, el Señor es contigo...."

He was already praying, involuntarily and out of pure instinct, he knew, as he pushed himself beyond endurance, straining ahead against some unbelievable force. It was as if a great wind were pushing him back, bursting right out of the *casa* and out of her flame. *Harder.* And the sound beneath him took on a rhythm, a regular *cadencia*, indeed a gallop...was he not running now but riding a horse? Or was he a horse itself, bursting forward with a human arm out, his own arm? He was a *centauro*, he realized, and in that last possible moment, as he suddenly was very close to her— galloping straight into the *casa*, unable to stop—his arm brushed through the flame, his hand took the offered dagger and held it firmly in grip as he was leaping with his horse-legs, pushing hard off the ground and flying forward, propelled by all that weight that had been pounding down on him....

"...Ahora y en la hora de nuestra muerte. Amén. Dios te salve María, llena eres de gracia...."

I must kill Señor Cacique....

Madre María, this oppressive weight, this terrible sleep, I must get out of it! Time is running out—tonight or never! Tomorrow we will climb out of this canyon and the whole countryside to the north will be visible from the ridge. Señor Cacique will no longer even need us. It will all be there plainly before him with the volcano in the distance. His *compadres* on his talking radio can direct him from there to Casaroja...dear, dear Lord!

And Felipe saw, for just a moment, the reflection of the moon in the puddles before his feet. He strained to look upwards, saw the moon itself, for an instant, before the weight of his exhaustion took him crashing back. But he had fixed its position: yes it had moved but not greatly. It was still darkest night and there was still time. If only....

He curled his horse legs close to himself underneath, so as to clear the *casa* in his leap, and they all worked perfectly, obeying his every thought. All that crushing weight shifted and resolved into that movement, as he flew straight into a...black wall...a void....

Light...blinding....

Darkness...but brightening....

Smells. And sounds, the tinkling of glasses....

"¡Este sitio huele a una pocilga!" The words burst forth out of his mouth.

"No me eches la culpa a mí," the companion next to him at the bar table stated dispassionately.

Felipe let his eyes open wider...everything was fine now...no more of that light. Shadows began to resolve into shapes: figures in the distance, men sitting around the table with him...his *compañeros*! It was their favorite *cantina* near the *universidad*, a long summer afternoon. Oh, thank God, Felipe sighed, greatly relieved, what an awful nightmare that was! What with that insolent peasant and that dangerous landscape, that monstrous intruder with the blue *pañeulo*...that vision of Inés as a flame.... He could see everything clearly, behind him: *it had only been a dream. Gracias, Madre María.* His prayers had been answered, after all. It was all as it always had been, in this place of safety and good fellowship, and there was no reason to think that it would not go on forever.

"So you don't like the smell here, huh, Felipe?" A gruff voice almost directly across the table almost barked at him like a dog, or a....

Cerdo, cerdo...*porcino?*

Felipe involuntarily gripped the nose on his own face...no, not a snout there, either.... Perhaps a horse's nose? *No...why think that?* Oh yes, he remembered...but no, a *centauro* is *human* in the upper half, so I am fine.... Oh no, perhaps not...oh no, but....

He strained...strained with all his might to apprehend his own legs...but could not, that terrible weight: it was *still here*...it was crashing down on him and he could not shift himself to see...no....

But he could stamp his feet against the wood floor, see? Yes, everything was certainly all right. Good human feet, as they should be. *Two* of them, exactly! He felt like dancing!

He saw that his *compañero* across the table was just as he should be too—good Ignacio! His familiar balding pate, his handlebar *mostacho* failing to mask his devilishly friendly grin. How absolutely ludicrous, that passing momentary illusion of him barking with a dog's voice.... Felipe saw Ignacio breaking into a broad smile, that marvelous healthy spirit he brought to every occasion, his strength of character, his reassuring good cheer.

"Everything's fine by me," Felipe heard himself saying, with deep relief, as if breathing out all that anxiety. Laughter resounded throughout the room. Felipe looked around the table, was heartened to see that everyone was here.

"¿Te gustaría una bebida?" It was Pedro, that joker, under his clownish mop of hair, fumbling around. Pedro, the one you could never quite figure until the punch line, until you were all practically on the floor laughing.

"Sí, por favor."

Shortly a black rustle passed nearby. Felipe determinedly kept looking straight ahead, did not turn to focus on that movement, and briefly closed his eyes. Then slowly opened them: the black rustle was gone, leaving a shot of Tequila in a clear funnel-shaped glass out before him, plus a fresh frosted bottle of Tecate to chase it. Now where else in the world would you ever want to be?

He savored the fine bitter taste, lapped his tongue in it. Closed his eyes, held the shot glass against his nose, wonderful....

Staring straight ahead, he let his eyes focus on that silver cross that hung on a chain around Ignacio's neck, catching a shaft of the dim light. It came into clear focus for him. Studded with turquoise, small squares of tan, of crystal blue....

That ungodly *pañuelo*!

Everything suddenly light, very bright. Sped up images of horses... hooves pounding...villages burning, blood flowing, soldiers....

"*I must kill Señor Cacique!!*"

Felipe found himself standing erect, fully awake in the moonlight. A fresh breeze was coming through the canyon, cooling his sweat-drenched skin. He felt as if a whole flock of birds had flown out of his mouth. He stood rigid and terrified for the shout he felt sure he had let loose, yanking himself finally out of sleep as if by one last great act of will.

The dagger remained firmly fixed in his grip, his hands to his side....

But no one seemed to have been awakened by his remembered shout. Neither Toda nor the *gringo* could be heard stirring. There was only the continuing guttural croaking of a single bird, far away now, all others seeming to have finally gone to sleep. The moon had moved again, transited a full third of the sky since sleep had first overcome him. But it was still pitch dark night...*gracias, María*. There was yet time to accomplish his hateful task but he needed to get on with it. And so he stepped forward, softly, carefully, out of the clearing and into the moist jungle, toward the one direction where he was certain the impostor lay sleeping.

Felipe felt his own breathing, felt his head clear. The rich smells on these shafts of breeze filled his nostrils. He sifted them out— rotting fruit, the burros, pollen, wet leaves—but no man, still. As his night vision fully engaged, he saw that the world at his feet was well lit for his purposes, the half-moon so bright that it did not fail to penetrate even the deepest parts of the thicket. Slowly, slowly, he counseled himself, falling into a quiet but purposeful rhythm, his wet, bare feet feeling ahead carefully along the muddy floor of the thicket before he put his full weight into his next stride.

"...Y bendito es el fruto de tu vientre, Jesús. Santa María, Madre de Dios, ruega por nosotros pecadores...."

Michael Morow

His prayer continued, fell into the same rhythm and locked into it. He felt fully alive, alert—fully integrated, absolutely simple. His purpose had stripped his whole self down to a continuous record of sights, sounds, smells. And imbued him with an equal determination and caution against making any such traces, himself, of sights, sounds, smells....

Moonlight limned the edges of leaves. Eyes fixed the precise space between them. He curved and bladed his body to slip soundlessly through. The handle of the dagger felt good, cool, hard in his grip. He kept it close and ready. *Go for the thigh*, he thought, *when you see him go right in for the thigh, an inner thigh on first thrust if you can stay lucky and clear-headed about it.* No bones there, no...foolish to go for the chest, with the ribcage. And avoid, too, any foolhardy motion of going for the neck, the face: there are two hands, two long arms, two elbows to instinctively block such blows. Yes, go for something quick and sure. Go where your smaller size makes your advantage. Of course, the *gringo* could kick you. But brace yourself for that: *and move fast, think always of his lumbering clumsiness, that ridiculous toes-out way he walks, rolling along like an oversized duck*.... Yes, Felipe, go for the groin: *big blood vessels there*.... Whatever happens to you after that you will have done him great damage...*he will never be able to get out of this canyon, then.* Even if he kills me, I will then still have been successful....

Where is all this coming from? Another voice fleetingly pierced Felipe's mind. *You never killed anybody before, in your life, never even thought about it.*

Well, he braced himself against it, recognizing for once the voice of his own terror: *I am thinking about it, now.* And I am *going* to kill... *now*....

These distractions...they came out of nowhere and there was a terrible trajectory to them.... Felipe felt himself dodging them as he was dodging the big leaves, as he was avoiding slipping on the wet canyon floor in his careful, searching stride.... Stay clear-headed and just move....

And remember that bracing, glorious last fragment of that vast dream, he thought...wherein he wore his *own pañuelo*...not blue, but red, covering his face against all the dust that he and his

Casaroja

compañeros were kicking up on horseback as they stormed into Casaroja, driving those evil men out just like in *The Magnificent Seven*. And with Ignacio's cross medal, miraculously transformed into a silver staff held out by Ignacio, in the lead, up in the blue sky! See this, intruders!

It was all a fantasy, of course, though he was certain an angel had sent it to him for inspiration, to rouse and steel him up out of his unmanly slumber. And he remembered Casaroja in his dream… Casaroja as he had seen it years and years ago. The bright red-painted brick community house in the center of the little plaza, that he had been told the first missionary in the 1960s had helped the people build. The little adobe church of San Tomás across from it, with that fine, small but clear-sounding bronze bell in the open shaft of the church tower. And the women there in all their colorful textiles, and the happy children, and the leather-skinned old men with their head clothes…. And a sound—a bugle! Piercing the air, filling the wind with thrill and resolve as the bad men scattered before his resolute brotherhood….

Another sound: Felipe's heart stopped. He stood dead quiet. No, *still* no man. It was that squawking bird again, though, much closer. Had something roused it?

Felipe sniffed the air. It was closer here, less wind. Nothing unusual, he concluded. And continued his trace of light steps through the underbrush.

Maybe I will find him asleep, he thought, *maybe I can slaughter him like a pig, a pig, a pig!*

No, Felipe! Banish the thought! The thigh! The groin! Felipe shook his head, tried to stay clear. But blinked: how exactly do you keep the mind clear, he said to himself, when you have never killed before? How? That has always been the issue since this problem first presented itself, has it not? How? *How?*

The groin…. He gritted his teeth, grimly determined. Perhaps a trace of a smell over in that direction…a horse? The *americáno's* animal?

"Gloria al Padre, e Hijo y al Espíritu Santo. Como era en el principio, ahora y siempre, por los siglos de los siglos. Amén…."

Every step the continuing prayer…*help me protect that village,*

Madre María, as my brotherhood expects…keep my guardian angel close beside me, keep me attentive to his voice….

There…yes…some distance over there, a horse's dull snort. *His* horse, yes, that distinctive sound Felipe had come to know so well.

"Padre Nuestro, que estás en el cielo; santificado sea tu nombre; venga tu Reino…."

Each small wet pool before him, in the moonlight, another bead in the rosary, another link in his prayer, his holy determination—

I must slaughter the pig, Señor Cacique, the blood of fresh pork must flow….

No Felipe no…what do you know? How? How?

"…es el vino de los ángeles…." Felipe heard his own weak voice, somewhere within him…. And what was that, after all, that he was expecting? Was that possibly a *prayer,* also??

No—no…. *It was that evil bandido's own monstrous words….*

I am going mad, Felipe thought for an instant, I am going mad…. These contesting voices…this recurrent weight bearing down, when these thoughts send me reeling….

And the troublous instant grew, and yawned…. He was slowing down, too. It was very dark and dangerous where he had ended up. And the horse's voice was lost, and the horse's pungent smell. *Where am I?* A panic of an altogether different sort hit him…the fear of stumbling unready straight into the impostor…or perhaps *the impostor was hunting him, under this same moonlight….*

"A sign, angel!" Felipe's uncertain voice, growling within him, was welling up. "I demand you speak plainly! My mission is true…from God…I must save those innocent villagers, end this beast's tyranny!"

Steeled suddenly—alert again—Felipe moved on. Yes, that is how it is when your cause is holy: you pray and you are answered in an instant! Bring that lumbering beast on!

Oh…no…no, I cannot kill him in his sleep. *I* am not a slaughtering monster like himself…in the *groin* only, then flee. Get his radio away from him, destroy it…we can deal with him slowly after that…he will even need our help, to save his life with a wound like that. Yes, that is the way to do it…thank you, angel. *And show me the beast, now!*

Bugles going off inside his head, Felipe knew he felt as alive as he had ever felt before. Every pore of his skin open, every one of his senses at knife edge sensitivity. Felipe practically flew through the thicket, exultant—

"Yes, angel," he almost said it out loud, gritting his teeth, "show me the beast!"

And he felt his mind fix the place...yes...about only a quarter of a *legua* away. No more than that. Precisely over *there*....

A large pool of water, a small clearing. Felipe moved carefully around it, the moon lighting up the water like glass. And there, clearly was...his own reflection. His own reflection—fantastic, his eyes shining, muscles taut and pulsing. An unbelievable expression on his face and the dagger in his hand, fit to kill. A killer! Yes...a veritable panther!

"Show *meee*...urghhh...."

The inner voice trailed off. And that weight that had dogged him all along, that he had dodged so far, came careening out of nowhere. And hit him full in the back, driving him to his knees....

"...Danos hoy nuestro pan de cada...día...perdona nuestras ofensas...ofensas...ofensas...."

Why oh why are my eyes welling with tears, Felipe wondered....

He dropped the knife, somewhere behind him...find it in a moment or two, he thought. Find it then....

"Como también nosotros perdonamos a los que nos ofenden... ofenden...no nos dejes caer en tentación...."

Inés....

That weight, as if a great leaden cone, coming down to cover him, voices rebounding inside...I cannot do it, but I *must* do it. I must catch a breath anyway, get a hold of my reason. Go through it step by step...confirm that I have planned it right!

"...y líbranos del mal...."

And what if you are wrong Felipe?

Banish the thought! It is he, not I, that speaks of the blood of pigs becoming the wine of angels. Pigs! That is how he thinks! How he talks! And that evil snake on his waistband—he is a *Diablo!* The Devil himself!

I have to think, I have to think....

And as Felipe thought, the muscles in his calves relaxed...ah! It was as if each of those muscles had mouths, gulping down the cool night air greedily, the fresh water on the ground. And the muscles in his arms, his relaxed wrist, that had so surely gripped the knife....

"Angel!" Felipe almost hissed aloud, "Guardian angel! Oh!"

The dark cone descended even further, unbelievably dark and dense, almost palpable. And a white hot burst of flame, fine and invisible, shot forward through Felipe's skull, started his worn-out brain fluttering almost audibly, mingling with the sound of that ridiculous bird....

"Kh-kh kh-kh kh-kh kh-kh kh-kh kh-kh."

"Kh-kh kh-kh kh-kh kh-kh kh-kh kh-kh...."

Felipe felt himself falling forward, forward, to the left, to the left as whole worlds split to fragments and fell with him, tumbling forward into some vast yawning void, as he and his *compañeros*, some still on horseback, some unhorsed, twirled screaming into oblivion. Angels save us! He gripped his horse firmly between his knees, reassured at least to find it still there, and felt that if he could only drive the animal harder, *harder*, he might still come through this pit, riding, propelled once again into their glorious cavalry charge into Casaroja, that fading memory....

But a spiraling trail of red-painted bricks, forever shattered from their foundation, seemed hung before him suspended in space, then slowly glided by his face downward into the yawning hole, along with some wooden beams, a brass church bell....

He shouted, tried with all his might to turn. But he could only see, high above, a corner of the edge of the world, its light attempting to penetrate far into this abyss but finally failing....

Yet, look here! Angels had answered his call! They were swarming like butterflies around the unhorsed *compañeros* whom he could see nearby...and these angels were grabbing at his companions' arms, their legs, lifting them!

Here came Ignacio...angels guiding him...a look of absolute bliss on his face....

"Kh-kh kh-kh kh-kh kh-kh kh-kh kh-kh ...."

No longer a bird's sound but a horrible slow rumble, somewhere below....

"So you don't like the smell here, huh, Felipe?"

Casaroja

He turned back to Ignacio but now finally could not avoid that black rustle...that long, sultry dress—their waitress...Inés, dear Inés.... And flying straight at him! A blue-faced witch! In full free-fall too, with that raised silver dagger in her hand, coming at him in a last gleam of light! *Agggh!*

Did he duck just in time? Could not tell...but cold shot straight into his back...luxuriant, to be sure, satiating his aching muscles, and that coolness was spilling out around him, too.... And that bugle's cry.... No—a *shot*, truly—another shot of ice-cold like an ice-pick, entering straight through the back of his skull—his voice stopped, all speech froze in final astonishment—

And he could only stare around to see, one vast, dark, black panorama, very dimly lit now...Ignacio, indeed pig-faced...Juan de la Cruz, indeed dog-faced. And that rumble again below sending up great clouds of ashy dust, and a dull red-orange glow from deep down there that lit the faces of the swarming angels...all goggle-eyed, horrid, tying weights on the arms and legs on his companions...rocks and stones, the blasted bricks of Casaroja...to speed their descent.... Tying weights on his own mount's stirrups, strapping a whole slab of concrete on his back like a pack, these helpful diabolic, fallen angels...*we failed!* A last thought, incongruous, but still willing to be amazed by something larger than his own eternal torment breaking open beneath his now horse-free, loose, kicking feet.... *We failed!* And that weight of all the world crushing him into the closing earth as ice-water spilled out of all the holes in him, his screaming muscles, oozing, pooling in the dark space engulfing him in which he kicked and swam...closing, freezing....

* * *

"¡Ja! ¡Qué hombre!"
A bellowing, monstrous shout, commanding....
"¡Hola! ¡Vaya!"
Splayed on the wet ground in deep darkness, pasted with earth he could feel but not see, Felipe tried to rise, failed, shot-through with terror. He had the feeling of an entire mountain on his back, of a horrible dark tower rising up right next to him. And the imperative

voice of Lucifer himself, his new commander, raining down. Had to obey…no! My knife! Where?

He lurched around fitfully on the ground, trying to find it by touch…blind…*kick* at it, kick it away before this demon sees…. Oh, what despair! So this was what hell was like—an eternity of conflicting inner voices. Submit! Flee! Obey! Kill!

The knife was gone….

"*¡Vamos!*"

Felipe struggled to his knees, wiping his eyes…mud dropping away from his body in wet chunks…. A shaft of light suddenly blinded him, as he stared straight into a fiendish silver plaque depicting an advancing snake, ready to bite, an etched script below containing words…. It must be my own eternal sentence, Felipe's heart sank, straining to read it against his still-darkened comprehension. But it was not even in a language he could understand….

DON'T TREAD ON ME

"*¡Vamos!*"

Again—obey, Felipe! He fixed himself to attention, sheepishly looked straight up…to…that ghastly blue *pañuelo*! Satan himself!

"Aha ha ha ha ha, aha ha ha…."

No….

"Buenos días Señor, ándale! Ándale, Felipe! Ándale…."

It was only the big *americáno*, quite alive, walking away slowly, mocking him….

"¡Vamos, Felipe, vamos! Ha-ha…."

Utterly crestfallen, Felipe wiped mud from his eyes, kneeling there in a pool of soft morning light. I have totally failed, forgive me dear Lord! Forgive me! The weight of my own sins is too great, holding me down. I am absolutely worthless! Oh dear, dear God….

The knife….

He stood up fully, sheepishly, looked around…there! A little gleam catching a slice of the blade…yet most of it safely hidden in a pile of yellowing fern leaves on the ground. At least the *americáno* did

Casaroja

not see it.... Felipe carefully cleaned the knife and then resheathed it. Then slowly, dejectedly, traced his way back to camp.

"¡Vamos! ¡Vamos!"

The thundering, mocking laughter of the *americáno*, some distance away, carried clearly across the fresh morning space. There was Toda out ahead, sitting cross-legged having breakfast. He looked up at Felipe, a sort of question until a split-second later the *americáno's* laughter resounded, again, carrying this far. The *indígena* quickly looked back at the *totoposte* he was chewing on, a rigid look of absolute disgust greeting Felipe as he came up.

Nothing was said. The *indígena* did not offer any food, did not even bother to turn and look at him. I am less than nothing in his eyes now, Felipe knew ruefully.

Felipe found his pack, scrounged through it for a few bits of food. As he went to sit down across the clearing he saw that the native's eyes did move a little, watching his own knife dangling from Felipe.... *No, Felipe thought, you are not getting it back*. But the native's contempt was beyond that, total. Absolute cosmic indifference, if that were possible. His hatred of Felipe was so complete that he did not even get up to move somewhere else. Just that face of total loathing, just that and the *americáno* beast's fading laughter within the jungle. Oh, what a day, oh what a life!

* * *

Morning fully opened into one of the most sumptuously beautiful days of this long journey. This canyon was very deep, very wide, and it took its time slowly trailing down to the river at its center. Morning mist filled it like a river-shaped cloud, slowly rose up and dissipated. At times the trail emerged out under a big, sea blue patch of sky, the canyon so broad it seemed like a valley. Greyish doves cooed and dipped overhead; noisy macaws squawked in the distance. One open stretch widened into a patch of scorched desert, the soil rocky where an old landslide bottomed out. Squat bare trees, strangled roots were offered to the oppressive sun, curled upwards into fantastic, gnarly shapes and ended, dead. Beetles buzzed around, popped into their hats and straight into their faces. The place smelled of ash; perhaps lightning had struck leaving fire damage here. High, high up above the great top of the west wall of the canyon, small black dots could just be glimpsed—buzzards circling—so very slowly from this distance, virtually out of sight.

We will be there by nightfall, Felipe calculated, confirming his earlier estimates. By nightfall, commandingly above the country. Where the *gringo* can see everything, plot the rest of the journey out easily himself if he has ever read a map.

The trail dipped again: gently, gently. And a constant gurgle and splash could already be heard, the deep river that flowed through the floor below where the landscape finally bottomed out into a fully tropical *bosque*. They were almost there, in yet another thicket. A group of spider monkeys whizzed above in the treetops. Felipe could hear the swooshing sound of Toda's machete out ahead, clearing the weeds and underbrush as they moved along. The expertly sliced leaves lay criss-crossed beneath their animals' feet, and the smell of mangos filled the close air.

Finally they emerged, in a grand, sparkling clearing full of flowering trees and high palms. Tiny multicolored birds flitted by just in front of them. The water of the river flowed strongly but did not look too deep. Silently, they allowed their animals to drink and drank themselves, poured hatfuls of cold water over their own heads and backs. Silently, as they had been all day, not one word from any of them.

But Felipe heard them: heard them in his mind. Heard the mocking laughter of the *gringo*, heard Toda's abrupt, stinging rebuke. Heard, too, in his memory the laughter of all the rest of them, raining down on his spirit: "Not cut out for it, eh, Felipe?" It was Pedro's cutting voice from the *cantina*. "¡Bufón! Useless *idiota!* Simpleton!" The place was full of laughter and yes, it finally sunk in to Felipe, the place has always been full of laughter, and it has always been directed at me. "¡Bobo!" It was Ignacio's voice now. "¡Hijo de puta!" It was Inés....

Well, go ahead. Keep laughing, Felipe thought. It does not matter anymore. All of you. I am beyond that, he thought, dispassionately. His heart no longer rose, since his humiliating failure to kill the impostor. But neither did it fall. It was quite astonishing, really, to wholly touch the bottom of shamefulness, unmanliness fully exposed for all to see. Yes—keep laughing!

For the blade handle inside the sheath, when he touched it, no longer felt good and cool to his open hand, nor brought any ecstasy of imagined glory. But neither did it bring revulsion. It was just the blade-handle, a tool to be used.

As they crossed the river he looked up to see, high along the west wall, a spectacular waterfall. They appeared to be headed toward that. Doubtless they would stop, water the animals again there. Most likely too, this very sensual *gringo* would want to take an even longer break, bathe and bask in that waterfall. Felipe was coming to know this one's habits and rhythms very well. There would be plenty of time to spare, too. And yes, the trail, he could plainly see, straining his eyes against the sun after advancing a little farther, led right up to it. And there, Felipe grimly determined, this haughty *gringo* would die.

* * *

Time slowed down, slowed down. Felipe felt himself withdrawing from everything, from the lush beauty of the day that continued to pass before their eyes, from the refreshing cool air, from the lovely music of the birds. And from his own boiling anger, the inner voices that he had let go, that had finally tripped him up the first time he had resolved to kill Señor Cacique. None of that anymore, nor any remembered visions of old friends, old loves, old places. Nor even the nagging meditations on the manner and the problems of Señor Cacique's death. It had all stopped, fading away, fading out. His mind was a big empty room, awaiting the quick play finally to be performed, its climax and dénouement. So what if I have never even thought about killing before? I have now. What of it? It is nothing to stick a knife into a man's thigh, then grind it in there and give it a good yank or two if I am lucky.

This wall was much more steep than the last wall, but the animals were doing all the work, anyway. And they steadily advanced, making good time.

Michael Morow

Now they were beneath the waterfall. They had been there an hour already. The animals took good long drinks, dozed a little, a well-deserved treat for their hard work. And Señor Cacique fairly reveled in the place, exactly as Felipe had figured he would. Some distance away Felipe had watched the big smelly bear, perhaps months without a bath, just walk right into the crashing water, fully clothed. Then just lie in it, as if flat dead in the rock pool. And finally rise, systematically strip, begin to slowly and methodically wash himself. He seemed to have some sort of soap or something, even a towel.

Toda sat some distance away, stonily immobile, having none of it. Nor would Felipe, although he made a gesture of washing himself downstream of the falls, but well enough within the *americáno's* view to fool him, to lull him into thinking that Felipe was having his own little holiday, too. And then slowly, Felipe slipped out of that view....

Barefoot, as the night before, Felipe again glided quietly through the underbrush, knife in his hand. Only this time no prayers. And no thoughts, either: only resolve. Knife into thigh—pull, twist...knife into thigh...pull, twist. Get right in there fast and do it. Catch him off guard, like lightning.

It would be tricky; it was important to emerge from this sheet of jungle at just the right angle. Still well shielded, Felipe scanned three or four angles allowing that, finally found the way in that gave him maximum surprise plus maximum protection. He peered through the leaves. He had come closer than expected—there was the big white body of the beast splashing around under the crashing water, almost right in his face!

Felipe backed quickly off. No, not here. Unsafe, for one thing, to venture out upon those doubtlessly slippery stones. No, better when both the *bandido* and himself were on gravel or land. Felipe spied Señor Cacique's clothes stretched out near some flat rocks, a short walk away. Better to take him there. No, disgusting oaf, I am not going to slaughter you like a naked pig, although you deserve it....

The vantage point near Señor Cacique's clothes and boots was much, much better. Thick tree trunks grew right up close to it. Felipe positioned himself there. Then waited some time. Dear, dear Lord, is the idiot even going to come out of the water? Felipe, his back to a tree trunk, strained his ears to hear but even from this point, the heavy crashing of water cascading down the immense, glistening black rock fall was deafening. Two colorful toucáns flew together across the lovely scene. He dropped into the high grass, inched closer, careful to keep down out of view.

Carefully, Felipe parted the reeds. Beautiful wild orchids were in his face; he pushed them away. He was surprised to see that Señor Cacique was already half-clothed—how had he missed that? There was just too much noise...he would have to act quickly.... Felipe crouched lower, crept closer, right up to the edge of his cover. His heart was pounding but he did not even feel it. *Into the thigh, then yank, twist:* this was his only thought and it filled all his mind. His right hand gripped the knife snugly, careful to keep it down below the reeds and from catching any sunlight.

The beast was clothed now, fully, though without the *pañuelo*. Felipe was about ready to pounce when, straining with all his might to maintain balance, his ears detected a drone, a voice. He dared to stare closer. The monster was talking, walking around in a circle! What was this—gabbing on his hateful talking radio with the other assassins, again? The words Felipe could not exactly discern...then he realized. No: *this* time the words were in *inglés*. How could that be? Who were his conspirators? No matter... one would not be advised to pounce him with this talking going on. His *compañeros* might hear the scream and the shriek when the knife went in, and who knows how quickly they could be here, then? If they were other *americános*, they might be here in helicopters in mere hours. No—wait again, Felipe. So painfully close to the rocky shore along the waterfall, Felipe remained tensely watching for his moment.

From this angle he could not precisely see all of the *americáno*, but as Señor Cacique continued walking in a circle he came at times dangerously close. Then, Felipe could see Señor Cacique's right hand rising, then falling...probably pulling down his antenna...any second now.

Señor Cacique's voice droned on. Puzzled, Felipe strained to see again but became only entirely perplexed. The monster held no talking radio at all, just a little black book, open in both his hands as he continued walking in a circle, talking. Obviously, some sort of devilish code book, Felipe thought—I will have to seize it afterwards; doubtless it would prove very useful to the brotherhood....

But where was the radio? Nowhere to be seen...though it *had* to still be running, propped up nearby somewhere. But then again, what was this odd cadence to the monster's dictation? Over the crashing water, Felipe tried to hear, could only get fragments of it—

"Full of...is the...now and at...."

And there he went again, with his right hand, as if pantomiming. *Why pull up, pull down an invisible radio antennae?*

No....

Clearly for once, Felipe had seen part of something else, another gesture he knew well. His mind revolted against it....

"be to the...the Son and to the Holy...was in the beginning, is now, and ever shall be, world...."

Felipe did not understand the words but had obviously seen Señor Cacique making the sign of the cross, repeatedly. *What was this imposture?* His mind almost went blank, running over many pieces of other things heard and seen....

"Upon the rivers of Babylon, there we sat and wept: when we remembered Sion:

On the willows in the midst thereof we hung up our instruments.

For there they that led us into captivity required of us the words of songs.

And they that carried us away, said: Sing ye to us a hymn of the songs of Sion!...."

It could not be...could not be.... Yet it apparently was...or could be, that heroic young man in the photograph; after all, it could have been an old picture. Or maybe they had sent some substitute *padre*. For what he was doing was praying his office. Felipe did not understand all the words, but he heard enough of them. This was something he understood...and it was unmistakable...and Señor Cacique had no idea anyone in the world was spying on him, no artifice was involved....

"How shall we sing a song of the Lord in a strange land?

If I forget thee, O Jerusalem, let my right hand be forgotten.

Let my tongue cleave to my jaws, if I do not remember thee:

If I make not Jerusalem the beginning of my joy...."

No Felipe, no! An inner manic voice's lost cry. *And what about that slaughter of pigs, those angels drinking blood, what kind of talk was that?*

But it did not matter, could not...must have been a prayer of some sort, too...I know not what...or maybe I did not hear all of it.... But that cone falling down over me, *that* was my angel...*not that lunatic bugle call. Oh Felipe, Felipe: truly a bobo: Ignacio's voice, in your dream, was quite correct, quite precisely correct. Oh angel you protected me, such stupidity! And so much else, oh....*

Felipe had stood, was slowly walking forward.... And had already dropped his knife, not even thinking of it.... Thank you, dear Lord, for shielding me...my own monstrosity....

The *américano* did not even see him, as Felipe came right up close. He was still intent on his book. Now the wet gravel crunched under Felipe's feet, squishing in the mud bed. The *américano* startled, as right in his path the *ladino*, his eyes lidding closed, crashed full force onto his knees in the mud and rocks, oblivious to the pain. His own right hand was rising above his head as he assumed the kneeling posture, then crossing down to his breast, crossing to his shoulders....

"Perdone usted Padre, mis pecados. Mi última confesión fue hace tres años...."

JUNE 1988

Father Matthew Eberhard, O.S.B. was at first astonished, next irritated to turn and find Felipe right in his path. Finally, as Felipe fell to his knees making the sign of the cross, Father Matthew was just perplexed. I have done nothing to give my identity away, he was very certain, and he had specifically told Professor Salazar to send him a man who knew nothing about the reasons for a mission to Casaroja. Those reasons were easy enough to guess at anyway, but ignorance might well serve as added protection for the guide if anything went wrong. Well, I should have figured it would all get messed up somehow in the translation or in the execution, Matthew thought ruefully to himself. And I certainly knew it at least by the time I found *two* guides on my hands, not just one. And then there was the jittery way this Felipe fellow had been acting, almost from the start! Well, this explains *that* much, anyway....

Father Eberhard gently placed his hand on Felipe's head, signaled him to wait a second while he rummaged through his knapsack for his stole. The priest then donned the stole, over his wonderfully cleansed and sun-dried shirt and dungarees. He found a good flat rock to sit down upon, and prayed. Then he made the sign of the cross over the *ladino*, and urged him to continue.

"Mi última confesión fue hace tres años," Felipe repeated.

Yes, three years, Matthew meditated...three years.... From that focus it was easy enough to allow himself to fall into that vast forgetting that was his realm for hearing confessions. That species of forgetting that was yet, on an important level, a special alertness. Forgetting on behalf of Jesus, once he could hear that always distinct little ring of sincere recollection and regret from the penitent. Each voice ringing in its own way, but a universal mode for all coming to this sacrament with truth. Forgetting too, for his *own* good, given the difficulty of being the sieve for so much dross, and then having to go on, often enough in these missionary circumstances with people you knew well, no veil of privacy. Have to get on, have to live, forget: and what a grace. But always too maintaining simultaneously that simple alertness: in waiting for those bells to ring, hearing them, and then momentarily throwing the coins on the scale, hearing them ring one last time, like a pulse. And finally, with each soul, hearing all those sounds together at last forming a unique pattern: the under-self of the moment.

You, at any event, had to take most of what they told you at face value to keep your sanity. Though usually, for Father Matthew, a question or two was usually appropriate. A question just a tad off-key or off-beat, as not to threaten or increase the person's difficulties. Rather to plumb the space in each person that might be available for growth, for the appropriate bit of direction and refinement of will.

"...calumnia," Felipe's thin voice came to him above his own yawning forgetfulness, "...dos veces...."

Ring: exact memory. "Bueno," Father Matthew whispered for encouragement. Yes, throw it on the dry wood pile....

Ring: *dos veces*.... Just as Felipe a minute ago had said, "hace tres años": three years.... The pattern already beginning to form? And one oddly matching Matthew's own....

Three years...could it have been that long? Back to the plaza on that hot summer festival day, the *conquistador* dancers milling and crowding in their combination of bold realism and rich, multi-colored fantasy.... It had seemed that the troubles were finally ending, the worst of them anyway, that things could more or less go on as before. Only two or three soldiers were on hand, and they looked barely interested and stayed in the distance. You still heard reports, of course, clashes here or there, but for once, it seemed you could be more or less off your guard in town. For although nothing had ever happened in Cañada anyway, you had well learned that you could not be too careful in this country.

Here came Alvarado now, and a very fine Alvarado too: old

painted wooden face, amazingly carved, straight toward Matthew's own face, bright green glass eyes into his own, pleading in their own way not unlike this penitent. But also, Matthew recalled, trying out a gruff, peremptory voice, somewhat muffled behind the mask....

Matthew had not recognized that voice, though obviously the dancer recognized him, despite Matthew's own mask and his banishment of his black Benedictine habit this day. Remember...of course. In a foreign country you were remembered because of other obvious things: your race and your shape, your walk....

"Atención Alvarado," Father Matthew had said, muffled somewhat too. And then had urged the fellow to stand up straight, adjusted his costume at the shoulders, pulled him up a little. All the while giving the firm impression he recognized the man. This one was a little short for an Alvarado, for sure....

"Bueno, Padre." The Alvarado dancer said in an easy voice that Matthew realized was Lupe, the little Kekchi sexton at the old cathedral in town. Lupe-Alvarado strode off, swaggering more confidently into his part. That is why I have remembered it, the priest saw: two men speaking through masks, as with Felipe up to now. Still however giving him a little encouragement, anyway, even despite the masque. This priest role is so part of me I do it in my sleep, Matthew thought. Ring, ring, ring—he heard Felipe shedding his sores like an animal shaking off water, a wonderful thing to behold.

And Father Matthew had turned and ventured in the other direction, to seek out Maximón, that saint and sinner, and to glean some hard intelligence about some distant and now dangerous places....

That was the summer that this long journey had begun, only finally coming to a close with this venture out to Casaroja. Had I even intended that at the outset? Or if I had, had I any idea of what was actually entailed? All 137 of them, count them: the little missions and stations that the order had established among these mountain Indians since 1961, when Father Augustine had first plowed his way through the country in his famous lime green and white International Scout. All 137 of them, mainly in Alta Verapaz...a great many of them in *aldeas* which had simply fallen off the map, and all of them greatly impaired to some degree by the tumultuous history of the last two decades, the revolution, the counter-revolution, and before that the earthquake and natural catastrophes, vast political and social upheavals.

Well, someone had to go back, that had been easily enough decided. And as the first appointed prior of their own new headquarters in Cañada, San Plácido Priory, Father Matthew was already beginning to plan his circuit of the mission stations that summer day, by the time he strode into festival with his own little light touches, a mask on his head and a native textile festooned for a sort of stole.... Made that decision alone and automatically, the criticism went, that he had come to know well.... And some of it coming back from Father Augustine, too, but what was to be done? We are still on a rudimentary level here: that was always Matthew's insistence, to the point of being driven into blue-faced anger by these young theorists they were sending down anymore—what was to be done?

Good Felipe, he thought, I have my own reparations to make. But I am not entitled to that gift of forgetting, at least not yet. And, given my position, maybe never. But, there is still one errand left, the dodgiest of all, as they would say on the old emerald isle. Number 137, the Mission of Casaroja, Alta Verapaz, Guatemala. Hardly the last, for it had been the first. Only now, paradoxically, the most remote, and in ways never anticipated. Casaroja, where old readers of our missionary bulletin still thought we were, they had run so many pictures of it in those days. Casaroja, where Augustine's old Scout, then brand new, had ended up in October of 1961 after he had driven it as far north from Cañada as was humanly possible, and then another fifty or so odd miles beyond that....

"...acusacíon falsa, una vez.... Borrachera...muchas veces...."

Yes, many times, many times.... Indefinite, but on another level deeply accurate, more penetratingly true than a mere calculation of numbers. Ring, ring: throw it on the pile for the fire, good Jesus, again and again forgive him, mercy upon mercy upon mercy....

Three years...many times.... What then was the precise pattern in this, what was the pattern one could begin seeing here? It is also only my own, Matthew knew, however uncannily my own. And for sure he had begun seeing it that first night at the pass, coming up to the crest line and encountering Felipe and then Toda, in their suspiciousness and fear. Matthew remembered that beacon of light when the waxing moon had first broken out of a cloud, throwing Felipe's silhouette and profile into bold relief. For Matthew had remembered that unanticipated pang going right into his own heart, even as he had maintained his own edgily cautious silence. There had been just a split second, especially as Felipe turned his head a certain way...that bony structure of his face, his prominent cheekbones and taut brow. That almost birdlike beak of a nose, especially as it cracked at the bridge....

It had been just a quick suspension of disbelief, passing to be sure, held in check by the utter seriousness of the present business and of the dialogue, the sign and countersign. But enough for nightmares. For this man Felipe was a ringer for Father Andre, for sure. And enough that, the next day, Matthew had hesitated to take the kerchief off his face, and the day after that.... For if Matthew could not mask Felipe, he felt at some level, he at least could maintain a certain distance by continuing to mask himself. And it was even a strategy for a degree of necessary control at this stage of affairs....

Many times, yes, many times. And in all the years, many days of regrets, and some days of anger, too. Anger remembering the one who, uncannily, had so similar a profile, that same busted beak.... Is this *my* penance, Lord? Is this the mockery You throw in my way, just as I am about to finish this large piece of patchwork on Your behalf?

"...He consultado a un adivino...." Felipe's voice trailed off, momentarily bringing back the crash of the waterfall, that great cool air. And it stretched into a definite pause...began to disperse into the realm of forgetfulness. Then suddenly the *ladino* regained his voice, his sure tenor: "Una vez," he articulated plainly. The voice, refreshingly, was all of Felipe's own, with an inner richness and depth that wanted to be a baritone, it seemed, except for the fragile, too-small shell that had to carry it.

But uggh, Matthew almost audibly rumbled, trying to maintain his state of concentration. Ring...but a hollow ring, a counterfeit coin on the scales. As counterfeit, indeed, as the reality that exact word signified. *De adivino*. Oh what You had to come into this world to displace, dear Lord, what still is not displaced! It was a rough spot

Casaroja

for Matthew and particularly disheartening to him, sickening. And something he had seen often enough since coming into this country years ago.... But from a *ladino?*

The priest tried to concentrate more on that awful, sick sound... "*veeey*no..." was how it had trailed off in Felipe's voice, with that precise intonation, just a touch of mockery there too. And then, yes, with Felipe's characteristic, very precise accounting also: one time... only once, but enough.... Uggh! But conquered, yes! Did you help him, our Lady, your foot on the snake? A little window of Matthew's memory opened, a couple days ago, shivering in a cave with Felipe noticeably clutching his rosary beads as he stared across at Matthew. It had seemed he was staring somehow right at *me* as he did it, right at and through my very center, Matthew thought. But by whatever means and for whatsoever reason, this young man had gotten the grace he needed....

And yes, good Jesus, yes, yes, how can I delay? Throw it on the fire pile, forgive this good penitent soul. What is that to You, Lord, a mere fortune-teller? What presumptuousness, what foolishness! Gone with a puff of Your breath! Forgive Felipe!

And, gentle Jesus of infinite mercy, forgive me.... Many times, many times.... For as awful an effrontery to You as a fortune-teller is, I would have been better off to consult one myself than to entertain such illusions as I have been led by.

Forgive me especially for this remnant of rage that still fires up in my belly, the embers of a fire that should have been extinguished years ago, years! That still enkindles at the snag of memory...my own accusation...his face, good Jesus, *his* face, accusing *me*. Is he with You now, good Jesus, or is he somewhere else? Or...somehow, against all hope and reason, is he somewhere still in this worldly realm? I will know soon enough, will I not? Yes, you will know soon enough, I hear *you* say, my old confrere, my charge....

Father Andre....

Yes, Felipe's physical resemblance to his long-missing priest was particularly unnerving. Yes, there lies my fury, forgive me Lord, Your own priest, my confrere. I would call him my understudy, if You had allowed me that, but here perhaps Your grace and Your mercy was shining forth all the while, I dimly begin to see in hindsight. I raged at it inwardly, his insolence, You know that well. But I begin to see, in his intractability, Your mercy for me. For Andre was never ultimately my pupil, or anybody's. Doomed to be his own, at some root level, for always and apparently now forever. And forever and ever, thought not quite yet amen. All his own...though he *did* of course read my own accursed book....

Felipe's small almond-shaped face, I have begun to see more and more each morning, Lord, is Your perfect rebuke for my teaching, for my priorship, for my idiotic book, for my entire horrible negligence. And if any doubt of Your purpose remains in me, Your quite exact purpose—matching the well-catechized exactitude of this *ladino's* chronicle of his transgressions—that doubt is dispelled every time this poor man involuntarily cricks his beak or sniffs, as it were, the wind....

"Father Andre Meinrad Mondragon, I presume." Matthew still recollected himself saying that, as he had walked out into the little white stucco-walled plaza in front of the priory years ago. Poor Brother Louis had been beside himself. "Father Prior, Father Prior," he had repeated, "there's ah...little, ah...*ladino* man outside who will not come in...and wearing a Benedictine habit! And he won't come in, just asks for you by name!"

And I smiled at first, at that, Matthew recalled, I smiled in my foolishness and pride. I had known of course of the great affair, but only *I* had known, and directly from Archabbot Kreidler, to boot! A secret *communiqué*—for the prior's eyes only. Father Andre Meinrad Mondragon coming to Cãnada! No Brother Louis, not one of our *ladinos*, not hardly.... And finally here, wonderfully schooled in intrigue himself or perhaps a natural at the great game, asking for the prior personally, me! Imagine that, dear Jesus, or did You see this cosmic idiocy too, from Your cross? My own horrid pride, and therefore absolute inattention to the newcomer's most un-Benedictine insistence to speak only to the superior, refusing the good services of a sound humble Brother. Why, Father Andre Meinrad Mondragon is come to San Plácido! So do you not understand, silly Brother Louie? Nor did I, forgive me Jesus, in my gross stupidity, failing to even mention, much less correct, that very fatal, initial note of pure insolence....

For who, finally, was Father Andre Meinrad Mondragon? I well should have asked that question, Lord, had I been an alert tender of Your Kingdom rather than a swelling, middle-aged buffoon. Who indeed? With that first name so insistently French, not the Spanish Andrés, for some reason Matthew could no longer exactly recall, and that baptismal middle name which he was even given rare dispensation to retain, speaking to some equally obscure but long, close-knit familial attachment to not only our order but our own special branch of it...the name of our foundation's ancient bedrock and martyr, no less. Such things and such families are too often whispered about in our cloistral hallways with an air of awe approaching holy reverence, where simple true respect is enough, and certainly due.... But there was the last name, too. "He's of royal blood," came yet another hushed whisper, not without a degree of highly suspect floridity in it either, but from the mouth of none other than Edmund Campion Kreidler, himself. Well...doubtless originally from former Abbot Primate, now Archbishop Columban "Jack" Wildenmut—truth be told. He who saw all, knew all, directed all—Saint Benedict Archabbey's very own Trojan Horse gift to the order, and Archabbot Kreidler's puppet master. Well, don't kid yourself, Father Prior—your own too, your faithful sponsor and promoter of your fast-rising career.

*But you were supposed to know better, Father Matthew...*why, did you not? Of course.... Matthew was astute and objective enough to know that this was why he himself had been picked for such missions, always would be.... The big boys did not know why exactly but were astute enough to know, in turn, what they lacked. At least when they allowed themselves to be guided by prayer...remember telling yourself that one? That was how it was supposed to work, was it not? And had I been more guided by prayer I could not possibly have fallen into such stupidity! Royal blood, oh brother. Yes, he certainly must have gotten that one from Jack himself, whose special gift was turning the charism of discernment into knowing exactly what every particular person needed to hear. How often have I heard that one? And even if it were true—*especially* if it were true—so what? Well, there's a sucker born every minute, one of my most astute countrymen once said.

So who *was* Father Andre Meinrad Mondragon, finally? Good question too! You might even borrow my old pal Christopher's term, call it the Ed McMahon question, Matthew thought philosophically, here in the dense jungles of Guatemala. Ed McMahon, that dry perpetual side-kick, sometime verbal punching bag to the famous American television personality Johnny Carson. Who nevertheless after one of Johnny's endless run-on gags, with no shortage of tall tales and "stretchers" thrown in, as Huck Finn so aptly termed them, finally just nudged Johnny to the point, usually an uncomfortable one: so what's the punch line? How *many* men in gorilla suits were there, Johnny? A politician had finally reduced the whole thing down to its very essence, in inimitable American fashion borrowing, in turn, straight from a popular T.V. commercial: *where's the beef?*

Nowhere....

Lost, perhaps forever, in the country of forgetfulness, good Lord. Along with this young man's sins and my own too. With all of ours. With his agenda, whatever in Your most Holy Name it was...with my own very stupid graduate thesis.... With all of our books, agendas, plans, missions, programs, priorities, theories, outlines, points for "creative consultation." Amidst revolution and counter-revolution, in this once lovely but now terribly poisoned society, ripped by paranoia and violence and revolution, with natural disasters as a colorful backdrop. All gone, into that place. I honestly do not know who was, or perhaps is, Father Andre Meinrad Mondragon. Though as You know in Your divine omniscience, how often I have wondered: who sent him? Who formed him? Who were his handlers? Who, to be more exact, was funneling this talent to Columban Wildenmut and his boys, and why? Or was Andre *sui generis*? Fully sprouted from his own invulnerable egotism, his patented gloomy pseudo-mysticism, all both nurtured and unchecked by too many lost opportunities for true direction on our parts, we simply gave him too many "byes." Or could anything have been changed at all?

Matthew could only remember, as he found his own tears suddenly welling up out of his own repentance, that very first afternoon, again. Nothing else. The white stucco enclosure. The short, thin man's absolutely clean black robe against it. That grim fastidiousness of him, first seen, standing there calmly waiting. Arms

Casaroja

duly folded under his scapular. And the way the head rose, the nose especially, as Matthew stepped outside into that space. Those dark eyes...dreamily sad yet afire with purpose. And those small round eyeglasses, black wire granny glasses giving him finally a definite nod toward the Ignacian model. Not Benedictine at all, really, except in his technically scrupulous obedience. Which was not obedience at all. That whole impression capped by the way that the bridge of the eyeglasses slipped forward a touch, coming to rest accusingly on that hook where his beak broke.... And for all of that, today I remember not a word of what we spoke!

"....malos libros...palabras injuriosas...muchísimas veces...."

Ah, good Felipe, Matthew pondered, did you know that you are a prophet? What wisdom here, in the petty dross of the world you lay at my feet! It sears and scars, but it heals too, your Godly riddance. Bad books, bad language, many and many a time.... This too for the bonfire, Jesus, let it die and disappear there into my own darkness, with Your power that You have lent me! All of those words, books, pages and pages...ring, ring, ring, ring, ring! *Muchísimas veces*, indeed, mu*chísi*mas—with Felipe's inflection of disgust. Aggh!

Every time with Father Andre, in those early days, every meeting was like a session or conference. How very full of it he was, dear God! Full to the brim, where did he get all that? Did he get if from us? At San Anselmo? *Renewed expectations*...Congar, Maritain...a sinful structure here, a "cultural impasse" there...? What was this guy, nobody asked, an anthropologist? Oh, and of course, the good stuff, the really top stuff...servants of God or masters of men? Your own old question, could you have forgotten, Prior Matthew? But how had that come up at all? Clearly but without ever highlighting it. Not as a subject but in passing, as if only to more deeply underscore a *presumed* shared affinity. As if yes, that was all there...only *understood*. So you left it alone, too. Maybe he had even read your stuff before coming, like preparing for an interview. It was downright embarrassing and you never once mentioned it. Never did your job, failed to bring it up and let it rot in the dark, in your own ghastly, festering mold of pride....

So you never found out, really, whether or not there was anything more than just an *appearance* of affinity....

Michael Morow

    So what was Father Andre Meinrad Mondragon, after all? Well, finally—face it, Father Big Shot, Padre Boss Man, the answer is pretty straight-forward simple, after all. Father Andre Meinrad Mondragon was *just a kid*. Barely twenty-six, if a day, on that day a pair of highly suspect storks, whom you knew too well for your own good, left him on your doorstep. Wet behind the ears, clueless, all that. And with a resume so heavy you would not want to drop it on your foot, about three or four weighty theses to your own measly one. But he had mentioned your own measly one, all right, oh yes he had mentioned it. Oh forgive me, poor suffering Savior, yes, yes he had actually read it quite carefully, I am quite sure of it! And we went ahead, then, put him out there, yeah. With very little delay, either. Our very own Frankenstein. *No, get it straight Matthew*, get it out *straight and true*, for once: *your* very own Frankenstein…. And now 86 lights out! 86 mission stations carefully grown and tended for 30 years. Over half of them! Help me, Blessed Mother!

    And pious Felipe continues to prayerfully recount his poor paltry sins…turning slightly every minute or so. A little tic to be sure, but behold the lash of my folly—this man Felipe has the image of *his* face, good Jesus, my monk and charge. Yes, yes, I am ashamed… where is that blue kerchief of mine, to hide my face?

    Many, many, many words, hollow words. No ring in any of them, not one of them worth a wooden nickel. Bad books, indeed. Foul language, certainly, beyond *any* doubt—not even a lawyer can attain that standard of proof. And verified by mountains of corpses, rivers of blood. There is something for all you theoreticians and politicos, all right, will *that* do for a notary's seal, an *abrogado*'s oath? Now let us proofread the thing and make sure we have all the words lined up right. Eschatology…yes, a new, and dynamically nuanced, eschatology…and a *praxis* of intimately integrated transformation, simultaneously and in tandem…new habitats on old foundations, and old assumptions critically displaced by a broader, more diversely resonant vocabulary. *Indeed, there is spawning a radically pre-critical consciousness, qualitatively and quantifiably, thrust into a matrix of hypo-oppositional discordances, a mobilization of pessimistic dogmatic determinism arrayed against the emergent long-awaited cusp of liberated anthropophany….*

And what was the matter with you, Father Matthew, as so much polyphonic gibberish resonated in the background of your own... er...oppositional structure? The Priory of Saint Placid, to be exact? Or were you just transfixed, bored, too busy? Where *was* the beef? And as Father Mondragon haunted the bright white halls of little San Plácido, bringing in the new game plan from the coach, or so he implied, where was your own *critical consciousness*, pre or post-dialectical, any old kind at all? Totally out to lunch? Gone fishin'? Truth be told, Father Matthew wiped his eyes, it was hard even to remember...how long had all *that* gone on, after all? Yeah, yeah, sure...that was about it. For if he got you by pride coming in, he had you by laziness going out. Sounds like the kid is up on things, huh? Well, as the old hands say, the proof is in the pudding. A wing and a prayer and a *huzzah* for the old mission house! He'd get it all straight once he got out there.... Well, wrong again, *Padre Sonámbulo*. For who was the tyro, who the tutor, anymore? Since this kid came in, it was all mixed up. And unfortunately, yeah, it was different out there anymore, apparently. Some kind of pudding you never even dreamed of, Padre. All mixed up, for sure.

But the funny thing was, in hindsight, how perfectly calm and ordinary, even banal to the point of inducing a sort of sleepy tranquility, it had all seemed at the time. All of it: endless. Yes, it was clearly all of a piece, nowhere to quite grab onto a corner of it. *The interview*: yes, the interview. This is how Matthew thought of it now. But of whom, and to what purpose?

The interview: a niece and a nephew in the States had introduced Matthew to the concept in the early 80s, when he was on sabbatical back at Saint Benedict's. Seems that a wacky new world was greeting those college graduates venturing into the American workforce these days, a sort of rite of passage between recruiters and corporate personnel managers. One stepped into this zone, expecting to be ready to engage in some sort of pre-packaged scripted play of self-aggrandizement. The questions they would be hit with, taken alone, were ludicrous, could even be taken as insulting if you thought about it. *Tell me about your strengths...and what are your weaknesses?* But really such "questions" meant nothing at all, were posed as mere springboards for the applicant to begin pumping himself in earnest.

Depending on the environment your tone would change, the "buzz words," as the kids called them, would be altered, much the way one changed clothes.

The interview was all they ever got from Andre Meinrad Mondragon, O.S.B. A little of this, a tad of your own thesis, Father Prior, thank you, a little of that.... Veritable reams of newspeak, seamed into his own endless, whole cloth theses, which were really all one thesis...words, words, words. There may well have been more things in heaven and earth than were dreamt of in your philosophy, dear Horatio, but what you had was yet a damn sight better than what could be located in the fathomless anthro-babble of our own Padre Parrot. Yes, that is what some of the *indianos* called him, remember? Poor fellow had no apparent sense of humor himself, that great saving grace that these natives had such a bountiful supply of. That which made this grand colorful country seem, at times, not only its own magnificent world but also the sun which shone down on it. And certainly their shoe for this particular poor mortal fit. But whether because of his own perfectly parrot-like profile, or because of that so very choice, individualized blend of pretentious academic blather and new age newspeak, it was impossible to say.

The only thing that was clear, Matthew chastised himself, was your own yawning hesitation, your doubt at how to handle him which, within instants, grew to Grand Canyon size. *That was over six years ago*, Matthew again recalled. I was still—as prior—brand spanking new.... At this distance the priest could not recall his own motive for hesitation. *As if I ever had one*, he thought.

The fact is, Matthew, admit it: you had no idea, in the world, what he was talking about. And worse, not a care. But someone did, to all appearances up to now, anyway. Somebody cared in a big way. That was the grim truth of the matter. And poor Padre Parrot may have been most clueless of all, about what they had baked into his vocabulary early in that upper crust minor seminary in Spain they ran him through in three years flat. Dear, dear, Jesus, as messed up as we were at the Saint Benedict's of my youth, there were even today a couple old hands there with eyes and ears. And sure, yes, they were still there when he had crossed the seas to our very own major seminary. Still Andre Meinrad was slipped past all of them, out of their sight. *Take him at face value, Brothers*. And we had. And all that came dangling from his coattails was invisible to us, perhaps, but not to Somebody. Junta killers or Marxist assassins, Cinna the poet or Cinna the conspirator, what practical difference did it finally make, after all?

Well, after you had seen the results and the horrific evidence of it for two and a half years on the circuit, it was almost enough to make a Hindu or a Zen man out of you. Almost. All is come to nothing: nothing, all. But not quite. Unless you were ready to deaden yourself to mass murder, and to banish the notion of any moral accountability for it. A more "anthropomorphic theology," indeed: and if a mountainside of lemmings is washed away in a hurricane, what is that? Well I, for one, am accountable. Good Jesus, my crucified King, bringing Your sacraments to the people, Your sacred Eucharist, matrimony, confession, the last rites, is just not enough for us anymore—we your priests need action and intrigue, social transformation and a load of verbal constructions made out of pixie sticks. You sent me here to spread Your kingdom, and in my monumental negligence I have connived at bringing hell to earth! Forgive me!

Well buck up, pilgrim, Matthew finally had to say to himself. The dead cannot bury the dead after all, *you* have to do it. And in a couple days, too, you may yet see worse....

"Adulterio...." Felipe's voice came through the forgetfulness, clear but trailing off. Another pause, another break in the pattern, longer than the first one. And the sound of waterfalls came back, crashingly vibrant, filling all the space.... *And let it*, Matthew told himself, this is getting down to the core of the man, at last. And the time for another sort of attention, on the confessor's part, the attention not of forgetfulness but of attention itself.

"Un infante...."

"Sí," Father Matthew said softly, "Bueno. No te molestes, pero dime la verdad."

"Sí...."

And Felipe himself now carefully proceeded to complete the pattern, that Matthew had seen beginning to emerge from his catalogue of infractions. Here came the whole story of Felipe's little band of brothers, their haunts and favorite watering holes, the crazy American Western movies they were obsessed with, the waitress Inés and Felipe's passion for her, their love child.... It was all very stoically laid out, much like the rest of the accounting Felipe had given in this confession; he had obviously found a lot of time to properly meditate on it all and his contrition could not be doubted. But there was another element of interest in it for Father Matthew, this "brotherhood." Obviously charismatic in nature, one of these four thousand or so "new groups" that Matthew had read somewhere were springing up all over the world in the Church. What were these people even about, though? And here, as so often, lay the real root of the problem—a view of spirituality which, at best, was totally subjectivist, at worst was nothing more than an added excuse to hang out with a bunch of characters you called friends, let the good times roll. And of course, no remnant of ecclesial direction or supervision whatsoever, nor any connection....

"Bueno," Father Matthew said softly as Felipe came to the end of it. But explained, carefully in Spanish, that there was something that needed to be discussed at another time, even apart from confession and absolution, actually a couple of things. For one thing, a child had been brought into the world....

"Sí, sí Padre...," Felipe whispered, struggling a little.

"Fine," Matthew said. He patted him on the head a couple of times. It seemed that they had gotten to the bottom of the matter and the priest prepared to discuss penance and give final absolution.

But it seemed that there was something else coming. Felipe was stammering, having a difficult time getting the words out, visibly shaking—

"...planeado...homicidio con premeditación...."

It now appeared, incredibly enough, that this little fellow had once planned to murder someone in stealth. The circumstances were rather vague, and the penitent spoke on one hand about self-defense, at another point about self-delusion and folly. Matthew questioned him at this point. Had any overt act been taken, any injury or harm caused? Were others involved? Was he still considering this crime?

"No, no, no," the answers came forth directly, obviously sincere.

Casaroja

It was very strange and almost funny, and it did not fit the pattern at all except for the exactitude of the denials and the clear remorse. Poor guy must have a rather over active imagination, the priest finally concluded, shaking his head to himself. And he seems a little worn out, too, at this point. In any event, no murder had occurred and none was going to occur. Dear Jesus! Throw this poor mess on the bonfire, too.

Matthew proceeded to counsel Felipe on the serious matter: the illegitimate son and his responsibility. We will speak to this again before we part, the priest reassured him. And if anything happens, find another priest as soon as we get out of here.

"Sí, sí, Padre...."

Here the priest gave the *ladino* a part of his penance, counseling him that the real penance no doubt would be the "work we have to do once we get to Casaroja, Felipe, I will counsel you about that once we get there." The priest then asked him to make a good act of contrition. Felipe obeyed like a child, a great calm and joy visibly enveloping him. He was crying.

Now light Your bonfire, good Jesus, let it all go away to the land of forgetfulness....

"And by the power vested in me, I absolve you of your sins," Father Matthew concluded, slowly blessing the penitent who, in turn, made the sign of the cross. "In the name of the Father, and of the Son, and of the Holy Ghost. Amen. Your sins are forgiven you, Felipe," Father Matthew once more addressed him by name, "*Paz!*"

Felipe slowly stood up, as if a great storm had visibly passed through him. Matthew looked at him carefully. The face and body were in shock but the eyes were radiant. Matthew stood up himself, quickly changed the subject back to their difficult enterprise, resumed the mask of command. Tell Toda we have talked, the priest instructed, and please apologize for me: "I was trying to stay aloof and mysterious, to protect you, you see," Matthew concluded, "And I specifically instructed Professo-...I mean *Ramon*...to send me *one* man, who knew nothing about me, to narrow the problems. Understood?"

"Sí, sí."

"I have no idea why it turned out like this. Anyway, I want to make Casaroja in no more than two days, one if at all possible. Then do what I have to do there, and then get out of here. I have chosen this difficult route, you understand, rather than the old road, to avoid any civil patrols that may still be out here, and also to avoid being seen by any revolutionaries who may still be about. Any of these people may well still be interested in Casaroja, despite what we fear may have happened there already—or because of it. And at this point we should send Toda about a few hours ahead. He, being a native, will not attract suspicion. Can you relay that?"

"Sí."

"Exactly?"

"*Exactamente*, Padre Matthew."

"Bueno, bueno." Matthew looked him back in the eyes. Was the discipline still there? Was this guy going to get the job done or was he going to crack? Well, he looked a sight better, anyway. And there was a fine new aspect to him—he seemed to relish being commanded! You lost something but you gained something too.

"I will catch up with you in fifteen minutes, Felipe. I was saying my prayers and I need to finish them. Yes, you're a good man, and tell Toda I call him the same…."

Felipe turned to go, hesitated. Now what in the world, Matthew wondered. And then the young man just threw his arms around the big priest and hugged him.

Matthew patted him on the back, "You're fine, Felipe, don't worry."

Felipe was gone.

Father Matthew found himself once again alone, with the magnificent waterfall in the midst of this wilderness. He shook his head to himself. Oh boy, he thought. But this had obviously needed to happen.

And yes, he said to himself, buck up yourself. This one is hardly over. Nor is the time come yet when my own sins are forgiven. And the penance will take some time, too, some very significant time…dear Jesus forgive me, all this folly….

In any event, the priest mused, a significant part of the penance is about to unfold. A very significant part. Well, enough of all this.

Casaroja

He pulled out his long, lined journal and carefully wrote out his missionary's entry for this day:

Wednesday, June 22, 1988.

Identity accidentally discovered by Felipe Cruz at waterfall. Probably better in long run. Heard his confession, then he also informed the native. Hope to attain crestline by nightfall, then hopefully reach the mission at Casaroja in a day. Some bad news from the house. Brother Pig at it again; Brother Monkey given appropriate instructions. Our Lady of Einsiedeln, pray for us.

THE DANCE OF THE CONQUISTADORS

At twilight, just before nightfall obliterated it, a view grand beyond words lay out before Matthew's gaze from the ridgeline. Is there anything at all comparable in your memory, he wondered? Likely not. Young mountains, dull green volcano cones in the distance to the far northeast, receding to darkening shades of blue as the sun set. And below him to the west an unbelievably broad plain, slowly undulating in waves of small hills and raised earth in many shades of brown and green, darkening too. Some of it segmented by apparently ancient demarcations of human cultivation, lime colored, then endless zigzags of woodlands setting them off, dense clumpy forests, thickening and expanding in the higher elevations. Some ancient pathways too, more noticeable close below but disappearing into the high contrasts of late day farther off, under the sun's descending orb. And over all a vast, faint haze, the land's great breath, rising up in the already cooling air. You might even forget the purpose of your being here and the hazards, wish that all of this tremendous country, and this journey through it, might go on endlessly and forever.

But sleep was already closing in fast upon Father Matthew. He quickly surveyed his little crew and the shelter Toda had macheted out of the piney woods for the night. Now that his identity was in the open their arrangements were actually much safer, by staying closer together. He would never now forget the face and the eyes of that inscrutable *indígena* Toda, on their first meeting after the Indian had been told by Felipe of Matthew's identity. Gone was the diffidence and the instinctive fear, but in their place was another sort of fear, almost an awe, finally a fathomless bafflement and curiosity. His grey-green eyes looked straight into Matthew's own, plain and unflinching, candid and resigned. Straight-lipped like the old stone masks you saw carved upon the Aztec ruins out here, and just that immobile, Toda's small leathery face was criss-crossed with many lines, none of which revealed anything except age. In this new silent intimacy that Toda exhibited since he had relaxed in Matthew's presence, you could see, close-up, the instinctual marks of an extraordinary alertness—ears that almost physically reacted to bird cries, eyes hard and alive to everything. That, and an immediate acknowledgment of respect to the big *americáno* who had managed to trick not only himself, but also the *ladino*, holding back his priestly identity all this while. It was the most primitive sort of respect that they shared now, and their eyes agreed to hold it as their own fragile secret: yes, we are both that inscrutable, both that absolutely calm and unflinching. And this we have, above this poor *ladino*, and above all *ladinos*....

As the day's light faded out to black, Toda stepped aside of Matthew at their camp, made a little bow. Father Matthew acknowledged the salute, with a slight nod. And only then placed his hand on the native's head, blessed him with the sign of the cross, and moved on to his blanket. The native also clearly preferred the new environment of direction and command.

Sleep immediately took the priest this night, as he knew it would. And Matthew felt as if electricity were rattling out of his head and limbs. Down, down, he seemed to plunge, into something.... Given the tough work set out for the next few days, he had hoped nightmares would not visit and steal his needed rest. They did not, and there were no dreams for a long time. Once or twice he remembered waking, opening an eye, seeing the sky aflame with stars. He just had long enough for a sighing prayer of thanksgiving, for at least this much rest, so far. And then sleep crashed back again, like a great ocean wave along a moonlit coast, with pieces of faces starting to emerge against its breaking foam. These images carried no sense of terror but rather a deep, plaintive note of melancholy, a song of this earth tragic and sad....

Here came the *conquista* dancers again, *those* were the faces:

masks. And the music was the steady rattling of the gourds, with the pathos of the oboe-like *chirimia* winding above them. Alvarado was no longer the cathedral sexton but Alvarado himself, in the blank stare you saw in the old dusty paintings in municipal buildings around this country, only come to life. The *chirimia* leveled off into a martial cadence. Alvarado's face brightened into a halo against the dark, charcoal colored curl of cresting wave and then disappeared, as the wave crashed with a perceptible roar back into blackness, the seeds in a thousand gourds roaring like the grating of crushed pebbles moved by the tide....

Matthew groaned in his sleep, tossed...seemed to open an eye. The sky was solid slate black. Had a cloud cover come in? No, it was another wave, endlessly long and grey, curving like the undulating shape of the crest line not far away. He tried to look closer to see the faces of Felipe and Toda emblemed upon it; there seemed to be something he needed to tell them, something he had forgotten. But the scene was inverted somehow, black at the bottom and the grey wave at the top. And then as he peered closer he saw that, no, Felipe's face was a wooden mask, Toda's too—which ones? He was standing inside the dark space of a *moreria*, dimly lit, and the grey wave defined itself as a whole sea of faces hanging from the rafters above, wooden masks for the *baile de la conquista* and for other dances, all the characters and players. And there was a musty smell here, too, not of any forest but of burlap sacks full of the costumes for whole troupes of dancers, stacked unceremoniously along the wall on top of wet straw that clung to everything, to himself....

Itching, Matthew flipped himself over in his drowse to relieve it. Better, too, to reach for those faces...so hard to reach out in your sleep but he had to do it, for he needed a mask for himself, today, too: one different from last year. As not to be mistaken for a player in *this* dance, today...for another reason too...the reason he needed to talk to Felipe and Toda, but they were still out of reach.... And then this wave also, in its turn, curled and crashed back, just as his fingers were reaching for a carved face that oddly engaged his interest....

"¿Quién va?"

A voice, out of that darkness behind him. A known voice too, very well known...why was it attempting to disguise itself with that ludicrous accent, much less speak Spanish at all? Matthew tossed again in his sleep...to stare directly again at the ridgeline...to see materializing directly before him the visage of the little brown-faced *morero*, thick tousled black hair and alert eyes, a clean pressed shirt of a good businessman and trader. It was the young *indio* who had taken over this establishment from his late uncle....

"Yo puedo mostrarte algo la tragedia. Yo puedo mostrarte algo de la comedia. O de la historia...o de la tragicomedia...o de la tragihistoria...."

The young man was smiling, all white teeth. And when his lips moved, incongruously came the voice of Matthew's oldest friend, Christopher—and in Christopher's cool Midwest American diction. The lips moved totally out of sync with the words like a very badly dubbed Mexican movie: *in fact, like a very badly dubbed American Western, and how did this come into your head, Matthew, and from where?*

Matthew raged within himself, for a moment forgetting his whole purpose of being in the *moreria*, confused and thrown by the way that this entire superimposed idea of a bad movie suddenly and out of nowhere had invaded his mind, but that problem was bottomless.... All he could do, with one deep root of his subconscious knowing it was a dream, was to will away at least one layer of this fathomless subterfuge, will that the vision speak to him in English.

"I'll have this one," Matthew pointed at the grinning, brown-faced mask just above his head, not unlike the face of the *morero* himself, "not to rent but to buy."

"Thank you," the man said, obediently, bowing slightly to the looming American before him. "Is twenty American dollars too steep?" It was still Christopher's voice, even more badly synched, but at least it was in English: *no, the language is not important, Matthew....*

"Here, *bueno*," Matthew said mock-seriously, handing over the bill.

"Excellent. And this face will suit you quite well. It is good that you should buy it since we no longer do the *Patzcà* in this town. Do you have a girlfriend, *señor*?"

And then for a moment it was Christopher's face, with the same, sometimes impish grin Matthew recalled from their seminary days together...Matthew wanted to throttle him....

"I am a *priest*," he pronounced, perhaps too vehemently, but in any event the demure good-natured *morero* once again stood before him, with his own plain face.

"Well, even so," the *morero* continued animatedly in Christopher's voice, the lips practically in slow motion, "if you crack your whip well enough you can win the landlord's daughter, run off with her." His smile was open-eyed and sincere; Matthew saw that he meant nothing by it.

"Bueno." Matthew bowed back at the fellow, with serious gravity: *continue the game, Matthew....*

"And here is a fresh new *pañuelo* to complete your disguise, Padre," the *morero* chirped on happily, "You'll look like a real *desperado!*"

"Thank you," Matthew said sincerely, examining the fine blue neckerchief placed in his hands, its elaborate pattern. The fellow was obviously delighted at getting a nice piece of genuine *americáno* cash. He was positively beaming. *Now cement the deal, Matthew, you may need this guy again.* Matthew pulled out a crisp five-dollar bill to supplement his payment.

"Bueno, bueno, Padre," Christopher's voice, heavily mock-accented, bleated from the man's brown lips, "And here is your *vaquero* mask, use it well...."

And obviously very moved, his whole body half-bowing, the *morero* took a half-step back and in a single, flowing movement, removed his own face and handed it to Matthew....

The pitch of the *chirimia* rose in the background...Matthew felt his eyes tearing up a little...*now he did not have to do that....* Matthew found that he also was very moved. That was the very root of what he had experienced in this country, was it not? The way a native might willingly give you what was most precious, such natural, spontaneous generosity...*oh how could this army be so cruel to them?* But already the gourd-rattles were reaching a new crescendo, this dream-wave crashing, in its turn, and the scene blurring quickly away....

Why, why? Matthew had the thought, which seemed very profound at the moment, that this badly dubbed and surreal cowboy movie, wherever on earth it had come from, was the truest thing in all the world that he had ever seen or heard...somehow it all connected, all made sense...yes, and precisely that sentimental at bottom...*why, why, oh Lord?* But Matthew was glad, too, for the memory of the *morero* finally retaining his *real* face, as Matthew had seen him as he waved and turned away. And that made perfect sense also, of course....

As the next great, dark wave suddenly rose against the night Matthew found that everything was perfectly peaceful and as it should be. He was walking along the ridge under a bright half-moon, gratified to see Felipe and Toda sleeping soundly. A good, cool breeze was coming on and Christopher was walking alongside him, explaining everything. Christopher Henry Gauthier himself, yes, grown into an expert lawyer and shrewd counselor after all these years. Christopher, who always arranged everything so well and with his instinctive sense of how every and any social situation worked, explaining about this professor and why he thought he would be the right contact and also the whole background as it was seen from America and by the world press. Christopher of course did not know why Matthew had given him this task of locating guides for this remote part of Matthew's own country. But with his good lawyer's sense and discretion, Christopher did not ask. He quite efficiently came up with someone, as Matthew had hoped, who was thrice removed from the Benedictines or any other close affiliation with Matthew or San Plácido by using a surrogate to find him, as Matthew hoped to remain doubly untraceable inside this country.... Though he also had not wanted his contact to be so *entirely* remote a choice that, if discovered, it would call attention to itself by that fact alone. With so many watchers in this country, including the worst kind, the unsuspecting ones who were being used by others, you could never be too careful.

But that was all obviously well-taken care of by now. Felipe and Toda were superb and it was coming off like clockwork. In fact, Matthew saw clearly for once, there was going to be no problem at all: *no, Casaroja is not that sort of a danger, Matthew.* And Matthew could see that it was all far behind as they walked *this* ridgeline, which was no longer deep in the corner of Alta Verapaz, after all, but was already sometime in the future: the long ridge that the edge

Michael Morow

of the Gremaux Hills made at Saint Maur's Abbey in the Dakotas, under the same summer stars. And the wind there, too, was blowing as ever, and Christopher and Matthew walked along, recalling their days there long ago, their adventures since....

Of course, it was funny, too, that problem of the lip sync, as Matthew realized when he continued to hear Christopher's voice... although Christopher's lips were not moving at all.... *At least the morero's lips moved, at least he was part of the movie, now what on earth was this?* But then again, what need for a mouth to move when the wave begins to crest, spraying brilliantly white, and when across its long lip of foam are written words? Black letters in Christopher's characteristic half-printed, half-written slanted script, clarifying itself with each hollow note of grinding stone in the undercurrent:

> ought to be perfectly positioned to safely deliver the sort of services you seem to be needing, has a good reputation as far as I can tell, internationally in his field, and....

> girls are well and happy as you can see with your thoughtful gift, much thanks—

> Sandra sends her love and says to tell you the time we were together at New Maredsous was not only way too short but way too long ago, and....

> heard anything about what's going on here? Busy as ever in the legal wars, but we're having a great time. Chandra is always a good man in the pinch and the business has continued to expand through his always surprising....

> anyway I hope this works and if not, let me know. Glad to hear the old monkey house hasn't gone under in the turmoil with all the....

And the wave crashed, washing out the melting words from

Casaroja

Christopher's pen, further connections lost forever in the tide.... And an even greater, more ominous rumble than ever before was coming up, far in the distance, a vast chugging and churning sound, rhythmed and eerily spell binding. Matthew involuntarily tossed again in his sleep...*toward the ridgeline?* He wondered, tried to focus on it and saw only a blank dark shape, a long curling silhouette... not static but moving, surging—yes, another wave, but a very, very great one. And once again halos of light appeared against it as it advanced. But suddenly, it was as if the music had changed, lighter and brighter, with the carnival tone of *marimbas* mixed up in it. And it was as if he was fumbling through the pages of Christopher's letter and a photograph fell out. Yes, there she was, Christopher's daughter Justine on the patio with her dad, wearing the *conquistador* mask Matthew had sent her. Yes, that was the way it was, he remembered, he had gone back to the *moreria* and had found two very well made, well-decorated rosy cheeked masks, one for her and one for the new baby girl too....

And with that happy sound the whole festival was assembling and Matthew was carried away in the rush of the people...*that* was what this great wave was, and they were all swept with it up the long boulevard toward the incredible, ruined, bone white façade of the ancient cathedral. One passed families in their yards, assembling for one of the two big armies of dancers, adults and their children costumed alike in either *indio* or *conquista* masks, with colorful suits and flamboyant headgear. One passed young men dressed as *conquistadors*, strutting about and adjusting their three-cornered hats, sizing up their very real swords, engaging in banter and swordplay. Natives selling fruit under multi-colored umbrellas and onlookers standing alone, smoking cigarettes. Some tourists too, and a couple of his black-robed confreres from the priory. Dogs and cats followed with the rest, and colored banners rose along either side of the boulevard, fighting for space amidst the low-slung electric wires above the stucco house fronts....

The tide finally broke as it spilled into the plaza, the human pressure dissipating as the dance-armies formed themselves in lines, *conquistadors* to one side and Mayans to the other.... The great drama was about to start...the great drama....

A strange, unreal sound, snaking up into the air...a vagrant, primal cry from the *chirimia*. All else fell silent.... Again....

And that tide disappearing, blackness closing in again....

Yet that note once more, higher, wild and daring, defiant, fighting against the void and those incessant forces that threatened to erase everything....

Then suddenly, all in flaming scarlet, Ajitz commanded the great space as his song seemed to reach the sky. Ajitz absolutely quiet, absolutely still as people fell away from him leaving an aura about his figure, to match his natural kingship. His sharp, wedge-shaped wooden nose seemed to sniff the wind, his bright blue glass eyes glistened as if fully alive. Resplendent in his fire-bright suit coat and pants, gold laced and buttoned, perfectly pressed and fresh, his centered stillness ordered all to silence in his moment, filled the plaza with a perceptible awe. It was as if his figure had been somehow ripped directly out of his own day, almost five centuries in the past, and had been projected directly here. From this moment the fullness and depth of this drama took over, its terrible grandeur only gaining in stature and intensity with each year it was duly performed again, gathering all players and onlookers alike in an invisible whirlpool of suspended disbelief by its sheer, stark visual insistence: us, them, then, now, always....

Ajitz slightly cocked his head, like a great tropical bird, turned slightly here, slightly there as if momentarily surveying each face gathered here: friend or foe? Sorcerer too, his kingly eye also probed. The twin green quetzals carved into his brow spoke of his origins, deep in the forests of this country's past. But as with so much else in Guatemala, his figure's power was compounded by a canny syncretism. Those epaulettes on his shoulders, just like those of the *conquistadors*, only crimson, were of an eighteenth century military vintage. And in the way Ajitz thrust his chin, tapped his foot while calmly making his survey, he projected nothing less than a strong dose of Spanish *pundonor* into the heart of this theatre. A martial drum roll accordingly grew, steadily, as he stood there.

And for their part, the *conquistador* masquers along the other side of the plaza were, with like paradox, most Indian-like, already shaking their gourd rattles against him in a great roar....

Casaroja

These sounds reached a crescendo as that wave broke, and all faces dissolved in it. Blackness reigned in Matthew's consciousness for a time, and he wished to hold it there, wished it would stay.... He wanted only to move invisibly through that day, once again. Move like a sleepwalker, safely disguised under his *vaquero* mask and his *pañuelo*, and with plain shirt and pants to go with them. But it was funny from that hidden vantage point how so many people he knew could be recognized here today, if you looked closely: Christopher and his daughter, whom he had never even known had come to Guatemala. How had they accomplished that without his own knowing? And there—this man Felipe Cruz—lining up as a *conquistador*. And there opposite, as an *indio* warrior, Toda. Even funnier how their masks were carved to exactly match their own faces...but no, there was no mistaking that as he peered closer at a myriad of faces forming themselves upon the crest of this next black wave....

Music spilled around everywhere as the lines of dancers came up. The happy *marimba* music once again replaced all. And there were little side dances, two or three *conquistadors* and a *torito*, and a funny little sideshow with a clown.

But already, so quickly, these images vanished too. Although a certain inner feeling of alarm remained. As if you had come to know that all was moving, inexorably, toward some direction you would regret having stayed too long to witness.

Now here they came: the great advancing horde of *conquistadors* like a moving wall, advancing steadily but turbulent too. They were shaking their rattles, their bodies turning all side-to-side as still their inexorable, unified steps carried them forward. The *marimba* sounds continued but fell into a rhythm to match the march. Alvarado led his army front and center, fabulously adorned with white embroidered cloth for his breastplate, superimposed on his black military uniform. Right next to him was jet-black faced Negrito, a gold-crowned mask and thick gold moustache like all the others, bright blue eyes. A rainbow of colored feathers flew high above their three cornered hats, and the sounds of rattles, *chirimia* and a flute rose over *marimba* and drums up to an unbelievable point and just held there, as if the froth of this wave was breaking in slow motion....

Still the whole impression it left, grand as it was, carried again that note of indescribable sadness—the source of which hit Matthew at the last possible moment. Before this vision, too, in fatalistic turn, was obliterated. Because just before that moment, he recognized, unmistakably in the second line of soldiers, the rosy-cheeked, beardless mask covering a thin Hispanic face. This *conquistador* was somehow audibly calling to Matthew above the din, in a voice recognizably familiar despite the muffling effect of his mask—Father Andre!

Matthew practically sat up in his sleep—then seemed to be falling, falling into a vast cool darkness, bottomless.... Very cool and very exhilarating, but dangerous too his mind recognized—*got too close to that breaking wave, was swept into some sort of undertow....*

But he cried out, audibly out of his sleep: "Andre! Andre! You're alive!" But try to reach him as he might, reaching backwards, the force of this last wave was grinding him underneath the tideline with the pebbles, sending him back opposite from the direction of the parade with the sweep of the undertow, all the way back up the long boulevard....

The cathedral loomed there, though he could not see it...he kept reaching out, as if to grab on to its steeple to stop, pull himself up and out....

At the last moment he saw the crack of a door open—a sliver of light inside, a black form silhouetted against it. Reaching for the door he found his hands on it, and then found himself somehow upright as he walked inside to a vast, coal-black room, churchlike but not a church. Hundreds of little candles defined themselves against this blackness, not another wave of masked faces but vigil lights in all colors—yellow, green, red, blue, orange, white....

They were set up in neat rows, he came to see as he quietly moved through the hushed interior. And somehow he knew *this* was where he was supposed to be, at last. This was where he was to learn the way to his still-coded contact, Christopher's professor. He instinctively brought his hand up to his face, felt his mask—wonderful, it was still securely there. And as the interior became clear in this darkness, he was also reassured to know that all the rest of his costume of an ordinary *vaquero* was in place. No, no one would recognize him at all. Except the one who would be expecting him....

Maximón, that burlesque of a saint, part remnant of an ancient Mayan idol, part outrageous clown, held court here on his raised, bright green-painted wooden chair at the back. Taller vigil candles circled him, little wooden dolls with faces of masquers, other fetishes.... The Mayans silently filed by in their homage, asking the impossible things they were still afraid of confiding to priests after all these centuries. Maximón, or Saint Judas if you preferred, or San Simeon, it really did not matter because what he was everybody knew: that thing irreducible by any historic force or belief, by wars or nature, by earthquakes or by years of crashing, grinding waves. And at the same time, a dark star formed under the pressure of all of that, hard as a diamond in his people's memory. And wearing a flamboyant shirt and red patterned kerchief, for all that. And smoking his cigarette, a pint of potent firewater in one hand.

Matthew had come to respect Maximón after all his years here, and he respected him now. Some priests centuries ago had hated him, and some still did. They had taken him on, with varying degrees of success. Overall, they had been successful in reducing his territory, so to speak: leave it at that. And some shrewd missionaries, too, had realized that he had his uses, if carefully handled—like a gauge of general emotional weather in the community, a bulletin board in the public library, or a "letter to the editor" section in your daily paper. See me in my outlandish, gaudy costume: see me in my pompous, straw-stuffed wholeness with nothing but painted wood for a face and with that cigarette, cockily and perpetually, dangling from my mouth: such was the mock-saint's endless, fixed message.

So keep your eyes open in his space, say good-day to his solemn faced keepers in this little *confradía*. Keep your ears open too and pluck a couple pesos in his can, to make sure he'll be back next festival day. Maximón was as indelible and native to this place as a lizard or a quetzal: pay his toll and do not assume that his eradication, even if you could accomplish it, would not create much worse harm than this little bit of houseworn superstition and irreverent play. The only sure sign of Satan, Matthew had long concluded, was a total loss of humor. In such light, Maximón was far up the road from that juncture.

But these were fine thoughts for the daylight of reason and wakefulness. Entering this space through the realm of dreams was another matter....

"Good day, Maximón," Matthew stated through his mask.

"And good day to you, old friend. But how is this? I do not understand. Is Old Patzcar hiring priests as his cowboys these days?"

Matthew perhaps winced a little, wondering at Maximón's directness, though oddly not because he had spoken in English, much less spoken at all.... Maybe that chief of the *confradía* over there is a ventriloquist, who knows? That fellow had seemed to wink a little as it had begun.... In any event, there is my own mask to shelter my expressions, Matthew remembered. Though there is always the question of voice....

"These days our landlord will take what comes to him," Matthew said, fishing for the connection that he needed to make, for the business that had brought him in here today.

"Ah. And you came for adventures, no? I see you smiling."

"Patzcar's cowboy smiles perpetually," Matthew bowed slightly, acknowledging the coded dialogue developing here.

"Are you ready then to confess the sins that you did not commit, but should have?"

"Perdone Ud. San Judas," Matthew continued it, in a mock hush, "por mis pecados...no cometidas."

"*¡Vaya!* Not even with the *Patzcarina?*"

"Of course not, Maximón," Matthew said, a little testily, taken aback once more by his prescience, "after all, I am a priest...." Funny, he thought, that this character's voice sounds much like that heavy, badly accented mock-jargon of Christopher, indeed *exactly like* Christopher....

"*¡Qué hombre!* What a man!"

"*Bueno, San Judas*, you honor me."

"¡Vete a la mierda!" the stuffed idol shouted, visibly shaking.

"My dear Judas," Matthew continued in a tone of perfect calm and modulation, "for you only the sins we do *not* commit, and nothing of the real ones...."

"Everyone says that it is so!"

"And everyone is wrong. People's mouths are evil: *no me eches la culpa a mí*. I have done my best to cure them, but perhaps I have failed…. Then again, that would have been a true sin.…"

"¡Mierda!" Maximón shook still, but he was laughing.

"Besides," Matthew dropped his voice, "real sins, yet to be committed, bring me here today. And I seek your aid. I fear only you can help me, honored *Diablo*."

"Ah yes, go on, scheming priest, go on.…"

"For the sin that I did not commit was to burn him, dear Saint Judas," Matthew said, "Burn my little gift from God that came insolently into my service one day, flattering me from the start. For even if I would have acted without justice or cause, cast prudence to the winds, or quite frankly and boldly just acted upon that malice that was already coagulating in my own heart, truth be told—in short, if I would have just sent Father Andre Meinrad Mondragon straight up the flagpole on sight—a good many innocent people might still be alive today. And certainly he would be too, although I fear he is not.…"

A little tear rolled down the stuffed dummy's wood face; he pulled a faded red rag out of the pocket of his outrageous shirt, held it up to his glass eyes to dry them. "Go on, my friend," he sobbed, "but know that this is certainly the saddest story I have ever heard.…"

"Especially sad, too, you see, is that I can *never* now commit that sin that I should have—that sin that only a person in my sort of position of authority, with a little piece of kingship—can commit. That prerogative of position, let's call it, that most of the world's people and all of its literature and so-called history calls tyranny. But which coldly viewed—from the position of the exerciser of such power—is indistinguishable from what all the same people, literature and histories call good government, lordly virtue, what have you. Only the effects differ, bad or good. I come from a society with democratic pretensions, you see, which pretensions now also infect my Church. I refrained from committing this sin, which at least would have mitigated a part of the horror in this mad, fathomless jumble of a country of yours. Preferring to merely look the part of virtue, in short, I sinned by failing to enact my true sin and weakness, and thus bring it into daylight where God might have used it to His ends, in the vast country of His forgiveness...."

"You have confessed well, false priest," Maximón nodded gravely, "Your old uncommitted sin is unforgiven. Go forth in turmoil, and may hell be with you always. But seriously, my *vaquero padre*, you leave me disappointed. For you had suggested sins yet to come...."

"Yes, yes, Maximón. Intrigue and disguises, an opportunity to create even newer risks, out where *revolucionario* and patrols may still roam, perhaps kill a couple more innocents. For over several years I have buried many of the dead from those days, and only one remote place remains.... You may have heard of it, a place with a famous red building.... But no need to involve yourself there. I only need a safe way to approach someone, I understand, who can get me there...by circuitous routes, of course. A certain professor who, I am told, you know of. In our country's city...some call him Ramon...."

"You have come to the right place, meddling priest, but there is a price for this sort of business."

"You already know where to deliver your bill."

"More than that...."

"Ah...."

"Yes. Nor to say that we have not noticed your complete discretion in all your deeds, since the days when you first came to this town, Padre. We have worked very well together, have we not? Both ends of the street, shall we say?"

"I think so."

"So just some more of that, no? For there are some new countrymen of yours around these days, of a *different stripe*...and I can feel the heat, at times, you know? For if they dislike your *santeros*, they despise me even more."

"Granted. And you to continue your end, too, of course...."

There was a sort of shaking, sputtering sound emitting from Maximón now, and he was heaving again, too. He was doubtless babbling his consent but it was no easy task. And Father Matthew had removed his own mask and was staring daggers into him...also had opened his shirt to let the dim candlelight strike his silver cross, just so....

"And the address, please," the priest insisted.

"Calle *de*...Alćazar...número dos..." Maximón almost spit these last words out, "and ask where you can find a new *rosario*, crusader!" But agreement it truly was, thrown out of course by the dummy's own will....

But of course, a dummy had no will, so...*no: keep on it now, Matthew, and do not look side to side*.... Matthew replaced his *vaquero* mask.

"*Bueno*," Father Matthew smiled, at last, once more under his grinning mask, "And remember this, also. I will not be so lax in sinning if my next opportunity concerns *you*, Maximón, rather than my poor confrere. So keep on killing poor little birds, yanking the hearts out of your pathetic pigeons, Maximón. But no more. Same rules, on your end. Or else your straw shell and all of your works will learn something of real smoke, real fire, I assure you."

And as the priest looked back, right through him, his mask's glass eyes gleaming, the smoke poured so profusely out of the stuffed dummy that you thought he would, in an instant, burst into flame...although he only turned color, as it were. The heat and smoke seemed to have burned his white face brown, the smoke to have turned his hair black, and he was not any longer Saint Judas at all but a caricature out of the Dance of the *Mexicanos*. A big beaked Mexican nose and thick black hair, big black moustache...a fine, pressed striped shirt and thin rusty red tie, a pair of classy suspenders.... And Salazar's voice....

It was their first meeting. Matthew had found the place, said the magic words. He had been disappointed to learn the fellow was what they freely and openly called a human rights activist, for a variety of reasons chiefly including the transparency of some of his associated groups. For matters were hardly that secure, despite all the pipedreams, and their mutual disguises only underscored all that should be safely said on the subject. This guy might be arrested any day, whatever Church or governmental figures allegedly supported him, just vanish. And who was he really working for, who were his friends at bedrock level? And how careful were any of them?

Of course, what else could you have expected from Christopher, after all? Doubtless Professor Salazar, a.k.a. "Ramon," was quite well spoken for in the sort of nonsensical, highbrow Catholic journals back in the States that Christopher favored.... In any event Matthew, traveling *incognito* again, had made his way down to Guatemala City and found the address near the *universidad* that turned out to be, of all things, a religious articles shop. He duly asked about their newest rosaries and was diverted through a narrow door, half-covered by a book rack, leading up a very dark, berserkly narrow flight of stairs....

Little light, but enough to see there was nothing...no doorknob, no other exit or hallway....

Okay, two knocks on the wall, pause, a third knock: "Ramon?"

And shortly a scratching sound and a blaze of sunlight, an apparent wall panel between old dusty bookcases shifted from inside, quickly, an arm motioning him inside.... A fourth floor corner window gave a commanding view over the sun-drenched plaza Matthew had just walked across, minutes before. But the very fastidious, slightly nervous Hispanic gentleman before him motioned Matthew back from that view, as he re-closed and locked the wall. Matthew saw the place had no door at all. The man seated himself.

"Good day, Ramon," Father Matthew said.

"You may call me Juan Salazar, which is my name." He sat before a fabulous old rolltop desk stuffed with papers and files, amidst piles of the same on the floor and all about this little cramped, V-shaped space. Matthew was already uneasy about Salazar's dropping the code name, and determined not to follow suit.

"Can I get you a coffee?" Salazar said, motioning Matthew toward the other chair, "Father...."

Matthew liked that even less. Stay with the game.

"*Ike*," Matthew stated quickly, insisting on his code name, "Thank you very much."

And they talked on for about an hour. Matthew had told him plainly what he wanted and how he wanted it: Casaroja, by a long and safe route, not the old, usual route straight north. No details of why, except that there were some *compañeros* to be checked on at this locale, Casaroja: where now for perhaps the first time in years you could hope to venture—at least some said. Matthew was careful not to identify either his order or his mission house. He had been grateful that Salazar had not seemed to have guessed it from either their prior, coded contact, or from his apparent knowledge that Matthew was a priest, made clear today. But Salazar's ignorance on these points could well retain a degree of usefulness, too; Matthew thus decided to venture no more information than necessary. The little rosary shop did seem an especially odd and perfect cover, at least in general. One might hope that the professor's greeting was a slip, that the fellow just could not disguise a certain piety. Though it became obvious how Salazar's conversation was thickly anthropological; apparently that was his field. He seemed entirely uninterested in anything having to do with the Church, an apparent unbeliever—though perhaps he was just being cagey, in this regard, if no other. The rosary shop was thus an even better cover, but the reference to Matthew as priest thus more clearly a slip. Was the guy just sloppy?

There was of course no need to say anything about the peril or the need for secrecy. The fellow was pragmatic and direct, and Matthew appreciated that, anyway. Matthew was promised one sound guide familiar with the terrain, native preferably, and the protection of his own identity and even his calling from that man, if that were possible. Also, if possible, someone fluent in Kekchi, since Matthew's was rough. Of course, there was the usual bargaining, and the sort of contribution to a cause that Matthew had expected: a few small, disposable cameras to record as much as possible…a count of the victims, their names if possible….

"Certainly," Matthew readily agreed, but withheld any agreement for his name to be used, in support of the organization. Really, could these people be any more reckless? And with the operation not even complete yet! Dear, dear Jesus, how much of this apocalypse turned loose in this land has been due to these addle-brained idealists and incompetents? He wanted to scream….

But Matthew had only grinned, implying perhaps more in the future, by way of noncommittal words delivered, however, in a daybright tone. Salazar grimaced somewhat. Sorry *muchacho*, Matthew thought, *and don't forget who's in charge*…. And for that, Matthew had to endure a little set sermon of about ten minutes length about unprecedented violations of human rights, which Matthew

Michael Morow

still found a funny term for mass murder, plus ostrich behavior from the whole world community and worse from the big neighbor north, centuries of "colonial dominance," and a worthy, desperate, punctilious attempt at documentation by some good people who were taking, still, some very real risks—

And Matthew had expected something of that too, nodded a serious accord to it all. Only refrained from any further words on the subject.

Salazar sighed, "Father, Father," he seemed to implore in his even little voice, putting on his glasses, "Dare I ask just one small, additional favor?"

"Certainly, my friend."

"*Bueno*. At this locale where you are going—and really we cannot thank you enough, we still cannot get anyone of our own to go there. So we have no right to ask anything of you—at this—perhaps still dangerous place, where we *both* know something bad, very bad has transpired...."

"Yes," Matthew had to nod, sadly.

"At Casaroja, once you arrive...might you inquire whether any there know the fate of...this man?"

Salazar had rummaged through his files, and produced a small, old, black and white photograph. He placed it in the priest's hands. Here was an extraordinarily young face, already dressed in the cassock. A well molded Hispanic face, yes. And very well known to Matthew, although not until a few years after this image had obviously been made. What a perfect puzzle! A certain blank babyish innocence, too flatly unapprehending to be called angelic, an ignorance that Matthew was astonished to see. Yet too that certain assertiveness, that directness already there, though still something very fine and noble in its youthful state...Father Andre.

Tell me where did you get this picture, Señor? Matthew held back from shouting, but fixed Salazar in the corner of one eye. *And a seminary picture, no less—where? Who do you know? Who is your contact in our giant, rambling Church structure that can produce this for you?* And...it was preposterous, too. Why had they no photo more recent, if they—whoever they were—were so interested? And why

Casaroja

were they concerned about Father Andre's "fate"? And who were *they*, after all?

Most incredible of all, Father Matthew was now at least certain that Professor Salazar was wholly ignorant that he was sitting across from the missing missionary's own superior. However he was quite sure of it; that, at least, was a relief. Outrageously but certainly, the house *superior* was a figure they were *least* interested in. And there was a disarming nonchalance, an air of apology about bothering Matthew about this business which could not be faked. Ah, dear Father Andre, who did you become that *this* crowd is so troubled about you? When we your brothers, back at the house, could not even raise you on Brother Pig's radio half the time?

Of course, none of these mysteries were going to be solved here today. Salazar seemed genuinely not even to know of their existence....

"Certainly, Professor," Matthew managed to say, gravely, and only at this moment removing that much of his co-conspirator's mask. Tit for tat, "Professor" for "Father." He did it as coldly as he was capable, though still injecting his own false air of enlightened concern, "and do you know anything about this priest?"

"Father Andre Mondragon is his name," Salazar nodded, "I understand that he was helping the people in the very village you venture to. Did you know him?"

Matthew was still looking at the somewhat dusty texture of the second-hand copy of a black and white photograph. The fresh smile and crew-cut, large young eyes, clean pressed cassock...already that hint of severely suppressed elegance, which only of course heightened the impression of fine breeding...a frisky young colt in the stables, biting at the bit.... Still, what bit, and whose?

"No," Matthew found himself saying with plain flushed honesty and relief, "I never knew him."

Salazar did not seem surprised or perturbed. Nor, thankfully, did he inquire at all into Matthew's purpose on this journey. He only asked, again, in exchange for his favors, for that little documentary work, notes on how many dead and any other information about them, a few photographs if that was not too much trouble. Sure, sure, anything...Matthew was already quickly withdrawing into himself, mulling over this discovered mutual "concern," and also considering this space between him and his host, wider than the world....

"I cannot thank you enough, Father. You will receive a message sometime soon...regarding the guide you need and other details. But before you leave, I believe there is one other thing that you should see."

Salazar's face was very close to his own, gravely intense. He had pulled something out of one of his manila envelopes on the floor, and he carefully handed it over to Father Matthew.

It was a black and white photograph, 8 inches by 10 inches, clear and glossy. Matthew held it in his hands....

Ehh....

Perhaps some sound had escaped from my lips, Matthew recalled, out of my whole being. I don't know, don't know...*because you knew all along: that has been the assumption has it not? And this man perhaps knew too, even before it was spoken: the reason you came. Exercising so much care, this good professor, yes....* But....

And suddenly Matthew had found himself before the window of Salazar's little room, as if jolted, propelled up by some force out of himself, greater than himself, having said nothing. Because there was nothing else to say....

Looking square out into the plaza, a framed painting. Distant figures moving as if in slow motion...Alvarado, in full spate, his dying horse writhing on the ground behind, from the sword-thrust of the Ajitz. And now the Ajitz himself, waving his arms before Alvarado, striding menacingly with sword ready...they thrust, parry, shout. The swords cross at their knees, between their faces, their fixed warlike masks.... But you are only remembering all that. *Because that was what you knew all along*: it had already happened, inevitably, with all the terrible fatalism of memory, of tribal memory, of the *baile de la conquista*. And what you are actually seeing here is the ultimate climax, the Ajitz also now dropping to his knees, his sword falling out of his hands, Alvarado's sword thrust through the middle of his chest and running clear through his back....

The *chirimia* rose, above the silent throng. Matthew found himself standing among them, as the Ajitz was tenderly laid in his black oblong coffin, to be covered with flowers and carried up into the hills. Matthew had come up close, to look at him lying there. Other than his death wound he was still impeccable, resplendent. With artful sleight of hand, his war mask had been replaced with his death mask, with blood streaming down his face....

Matthew looked at his watch as the music died and they took him away: three in the afternoon....

There was a general dispersal, amid a rather heavy, grey pall. It seemed that clouds had come in and it was already much later in the day. But it was not over yet, just an interregnum until the new final act that had started appearing in the last ten years: the death of Alvarado.

He found himself carried away in that misty air...seemed to be walking along the crest line again...where all out ahead and below was grey too, under the same flat, uniform pall. There were no sounds; the shrouded sea was calm. It seemed he half heard Christopher's voice, very fast, mincing and mocking, in the far distance as if behind it all...funny how Christopher had done all the voices. Matthew seemed to see Maximón briefly materialize out of the haze in his gaudy, outrageous suit, but this illusion too faded away...the stuffed mannequin had properly returned to silence, though ultimately in some monumental, staring shape, deep in the jungle...deep where he had once been born. Was this grey stillness very early morning? Matthew turned in his sleep, restless. No, it seemed his body demanded insistently, more rest: *it is all running forever as background and you cannot turn it off, you are not getting enough rest.* And so he turned, like a diver, and plunged into the next black wave that shortly rose before him.

Thankfully, a total blackness seemed to reign for a long time. It finally fully restored him at some deep level. Down, down...and still that ventriloquist's trick far down underneath it all.... But no, he realized, it was not Christopher's voice but that other's. The other who had drawn him into this final journey, his own wayward confrere.

Here he came now. Yes, despite the *conquistador* mask you could see it was unquestionably Father Andre's shape, his quick stride. For once Matthew found himself grinning widely to see him, some aspect of silent era comedy for once plainly apparent in the fellow. Still in complete *conquistador* costume, delicate embroidery suggesting steel armor. I do not know how it is you are here, Matthew mused, but I will speak to you, Father Andre Meinrad Mondragon....

And Father Mondragon, apparently having spied Matthew's approach, was waving an arm and beckoning Matthew to follow.

They turned into the darkening streets and corners of the *barrio*, off the plaza and the main streets. It was darkening even more, a vast final cloud cover having come in at late day, and a light cool wind had arisen. It looked like it was about to rain, but no one was leaving yet. Father Andre strode confidently ahead, talking continuously it seemed, though Matthew could for some reason hear hardly any of it. Andre would turn back to Matthew now and then and flash that smiling mask's face, then turn and stride on under that sweeping, black embroidered robe that covered his narrow shoulders like a cape, the tassels from the back of his boat-like, black three-cornered hat blowing in the wind, along with the gold, ringed curls of his wig under it.

Most oddly, Andre was smoking incessantly, sticking cigarettes through a hole where the mouth was in his mask. Matthew had never known Andre to have this nervous habit, nor for that matter to be this incessantly chatty—indeed, quite the opposite. But it was funny, too, rather charming and endearing. Matthew figured that the years at Casaroja, or wherever Andre had been since last heard from, must have been tough ones. He was just glad to have him back in the fold, if you could call it that when you were doing all you could to keep up with him along these endless, serpentine ways and turns, nooks and crannies of the town.

Gabby, yes.... Out of his memory, Matthew remembered, years back, very formal young men from Madrid, Father Andre's friends, appearing in the courtyard of San Plácido, asking for "Gabby" in their open, boyish way, as if Matthew had known and shared the joke. Yes, his Saint Benedict's schoolmates Esteban and Bernardo had also called him that, though more sheepishly, Matthew recalled. He felt heartened to be accepted at this intimate level by his charge, for once, to at last be in on it. Such was the strange power of the diffident fellow.

"What a world you have here, Prior Matthew," Father Andre

was saying, as Matthew found himself striding straight alongside of him, "Do you realize how blessed you are?" There was a rusty old wall they were passing, just a piece of corrugated steel, disintegrating into orange-red flakes plastered with posters of various sorts...public health messages in Spanish and in Kekchi... rock and roll musicians...Our Lady of Guadalupe...an *Indiana Jones* poster in Spanish with a somewhat manic face of Harrison Ford.... Young men congregated here, smoking too, wearing baseball caps, tossing coins.... Laundry and electric wires draped close overhead, doorways led up or down to apartments.... A riot of competing smells good and horrid....

Matthew had started to say something in reply, vaguely, "I think I know what you mean...."

But Father Andre went on, as if lost in his own world, gesticulating, his head bobbing so that the beaklike profile of his rosy wood nose twittered like a bird, "This riot of colors, the smells, I *miss* all that...."

"Sure...." Again, Matthew felt he *knew* what Andre meant, though he also felt oddly unable to articulate it. Matthew even actually *knew* what Andre was talking about.... He picked out the smell of rotting fruit, dog dung, fresh-baked *tortillas* in these weird side streets and corners, years and decades of human grime, sweat, competing sonatas of garbage wafting into the gentle, late afternoon air....

"That *infinite openness* of the human spirit, that's what it is," the mask-head bobbed, nodding determinedly, Father Andre's free arm reaching out to both illustrate and embrace, "the entire, rich social praxis bubbling up, struggling through junk and disgrace, stone and wire, toward its own maturity. Transforming itself every step of the way, *above* the dialectic, *above* both denunciation and annunciation. Verified by the dynamics of each living moment, *here*, in this slum... *here today* in this drama. And in your drama and my drama, Father Prior Matthew, all that we had and all that still continues...."

Matthew found himself just nodding, again *feeling* as if he suddenly understood it all. Though without the slightest knowledge of what this was all about, or if knowledge had anything to do with it.

"Ah! My friend! You still have it all! You still have all this on 'your plate,' as you liked to say, before you! You always held back, Father

Prior Matthew, don't you see? This is your own back yard, less than two miles from the little garden of San Plácido...."

Father Andre was facing him almost directly. Matthew found himself staring into those sparkling blue glass eyes, as if they were actually welling with tears, as if they themselves were about to speak....

Suddenly, there was nothing else to say. They both knew it. It had all gone suddenly darker; people showed signs of moving away. It was about to begin again, the drama's finale. And suddenly Father Andre was embracing him, both arms around Matthew, hugging him. It was so unexpected and unusual, having never happened before, that it had to be true. All Matthew could do was embrace him, in turn, pat his back.

"You have done well in everything, Father Prior Matthew," Andre's twice-muffled voice could be heard against his breast, "please accept my apologies. There was nothing I could say in those days. Please forgive me, and pray for me...."

Yes, of course, sure, it all made sense now....

Father Andre had stepped back a little from Matthew, rather formally stiffened, dusting himself off as if about to resume his part....

"Alvarado will die at six," Andre stated, unemotionally.

"Yes...."

"...and I with him."

Andre reached under the wide arm of his cape and produced his death mask. Wooden eyelids fixed closed, the brightly painted blood ran down straight from the crown, in several long streams recalling old medieval carvings of Christ's passion. He handed it over to Matthew, who took it.

Suddenly, Father Andre was gone, vanished.

Matthew found himself standing there looking somewhat inquisitively at the object, turning it over in his hands. Odd that this new twist in the drama had such an old, deep brown patina inside; the *morero* must have painted over an old mask....

It looked and felt in his hands like a half-shell of an old coconut found on the beach, light, its cracked edges worn smooth by the waves....

CASAROJA

It was late afternoon, and shadows lengthened along the widening trail. The hoof prints of the two burros ahead of him stood out clearly on the moist rust red earth, between some broad leaves blown down and pressed flat. For the last few hours human footprints also were to be seen, as they began to pass some of the settlements on the outskirts of Casaroja. The contrast between the shadows and the ground heightened as the sun, invisible behind the forest, brightened for a while. A few colorful tulips broke the underbrush. Then the shadow-line became very indistinct, as a full cloud cover settled in and daylight waned.

They had set out early and everything had proceeded very smoothly. It was apparent now that they would be safe, at least if they kept their stay at the old mission short. This is exactly what Matthew planned to do, intending to be already out of the village no later than two nights from now, whatever happened. Toda had talked to some of the first natives they had encountered, and had been informed that neither soldiers, nor revolutionaries, nor civil patrols or gun-carrying men of any sort had been seen in this area for almost three years. This was consistent with almost everything Father Matthew had found and heard to date, that the worst and most intense horrors had occurred mainly in the next state west, Quiché. But they were practically on the border here, and you could not be too careful. He kept Toda holding on to his own original plan, to start out earlier in the day and stay some miles ahead, occasionally doubling back to discuss the outlook. Other than what was obvious from the faces of the people, Toda reported, nothing was out of the ordinary, at least today.

The faces of the Kekchi here, though, told you everything you needed to know, Matthew thought grimly. In the very littlest children, up to the age of about four or five, it was not much different than it had ever been. There was the normal human startle reflex at strange men on burros and horseback, but still that ordinary note of curiosity too. They would turn to their mothers and hold them fast, but then slightly turn back toward you in the end and flash that bit of bright eyed wonder and alertness, even openness. Yet, a clear demarcation set in precisely at later ages, all the way up and through the very oldest people, many of whom doubtless had seen several foreigners or strangers one time or another, likely even Matthew himself years back.

In these faces you encountered what could only be called terror absolute. In the oldest there was even a stiff-necked, silent anger and resentment that Matthew had at times come to encounter in his several years' journeys since the madness. That glare was cold as steel, fixed and unblinking. The older children and young adults quickly disappeared altogether, leaving only these shell-shocked guardians as quiet testimony to the monstrosities that had been set loose out here.

The earlier breeze had died away and Matthew felt very sticky. There was also the problem, he thought ruefully, that although he had slept a long time he had not woken up feeling truly rested. Rather, there had seemed an endless matrix of complicated, haunting dreams that, if not truly nightmares, had left him shaky and drained. He could remember very little of it at all—a mask or two from the *baile de la conquista*, the incongruous impression of a long beach at night and the sound of the sea, churning against the shore. But he did remember clearly that small picture of young Father Mondragon that Salazar had, and even worse, that larger photograph.

Had Salazar even shown him that? Where did that come from? His tired, restless mind ran over this question as he moved along the forest path atop his mount, following the wet imprints of the burros. But he realized that he *had* indeed seen the picture before; it was just that he must have immediately, deeply suppressed it. It was an 8 by 10 glossy, black and white, taken inside a well-known room. The sculpted adobe wall at the end of the view curved toward its peak. A large crucifix was mounted in the center there, just under the eaves through which daylight broke through. Daylight also streamed in across the white floor and white walls, in angles reflecting the shapes of the rows of slatted windows along the east side. There had once been many picnic tables filling out the interior space, but now there were only two, in the foreground, and two soldiers staring straight at the photographer. One, in camouflage pants and shirt, very young with thick black hair and a somewhat frightened expression, sat atop a table facing the viewer with a sub machine gun resting in his arms. The second stood sneeringly at the left, right before the camera, in camouflage pants and an undershirt with his division's monogram. A beret was tipped cockily on his head. One arm was crooked arrogantly at his side, the other leaned against the wall as if he owned the place, as his lip fell open and his eyes narrowed at you with an expression of great contempt.

Father Matthew had recognized the place immediately. It was the interior of the community hall adjoining the church at Casaroja.

There was no knowing when that picture had been taken. Likely as early as 1983 but even possibly in the mid 1980s. There had been no communication whatsoever with the mission for that long, over five full years. Once or twice something had come in allegedly from or about Father Andre, indirectly and two steps removed, but all such *communiqués* proved to be false alarms, quite possibly even taunts or traps. It had been hinted once that he was hiding out with a Dominican mission some miles west in Quiché; another time it was said he had joined the revolutionaries in a mountain hideout in Alta Verapaz. There was never a follow-up to any of these messages, and they always turned out to be based upon some phantom source.

Occasionally too, something clearer came in: Casaroja had been wiped out; "it is no more." Well, we could have figured that out by now after two years, Matthew remembered himself growling to Brother Pig, the radio man, in about 1985, tell me something I don't know. Matthew had finally been getting ready for his journeys to all the *aldeas* and mission stations and wanted hard information, not legends. And why, why, he recalled himself virtually shouting on another occasion, why am I learning all this about "the famous Casaroja," as if it had been some important stronghold or military objective? Who was it famous to, and why? And why should anyone have cared about it except for us? And he could still remember poor Brother Pig's open and shocked expression, his total innocence, as if astonished that Prior Matthew just did not know. "Why, because it's 'Red House,' *Red* House…" Brother Pig had stated, in all abject sincerity.

"Yeah, right," Matthew had replied dryly. He remembered how his nerves had tightened immediately as the preposterous connotation hit him. As if yes, I had known all along, so what, is that all you have to tell me? But he had never even thought of that connotation before—although he had quickly flashed Brother Pig a glare and a curled lip saying just the opposite. He would have to ponder *this* one awhile, for sure. And Brother Pig's aura of common knowledge of such things, too…. But for now, fine, good, keep at it, Brother Pig. And Matthew had abruptly turned and walked away.

Red House….

It must have been about then that all this business about Brother Pig had started, too, Matthew recalled, and I had just gotten drawn into it. Perhaps the poor kid was nothing but a big fat American oddball weaned on too much T.V. and hot dogs, who knows? As such he had his uses too, for sure, uses that some of his more apparently pious confreres lacked. But it could become really maddening at times. Matthew had asked him once to plot out on a map all the known centers of revolutionary activity or Communist infiltration in the area, and their proximity to Casaroja and those chapels closely connected to it. Brother Pig had done this well, but it had taken him an awful long time, Matthew recalled, for someone always boasting of so much inside stuff. Or perhaps undertaking something that involved writing and thinking, something beyond just plugging some earphones on his head or staring at a picture screen, was way too much for our baby boy—an innocent explanation. For there always was an innocent explanation, when it came to Brother Pig….

On a deeper level, Matthew cursed himself for even entertaining suspicions—about Andre, about this outrageous *americáno inocente*, the Pig, about any of them. Sure, with war and chaos and a real live apocalypse a lot of it doubtless came with the territory. But still, *I am the prior*…I have that responsibility. And I am a spiritual father,

Casaroja

too.... Saint Benedict's rule, of course, had something directly on point to say of this—

> The abbot should ever be mindful that at the dread judgment of God there will be an inquiry both as to his teaching and the obedience of his disciples. Let the abbot know that any lack of goodness, which the master of the family shall find in his flock, will be accounted the shepherd's fault.

Well, enough of all this, now. Get into this town today and get out pronto. That was the way it was going to have to be. Do the drill. After several dozens of these reconnaissance operations you could do it in your sleep. Yet Casaroja was different in many ways and for many reasons, of course. For one thing, it was a major mission center, not just a little chapel, shrine, or station. It had originally been the prime location from which Father Augustine had set to work in this country in the 1960s. Many natives, especially, still viewed it as the mission headquarters. What did they care, after all, about our own shifting bases of operation and evolving organizational charts? And whoever had taken it out may have known that, too. And also known that many of the stations and little chapels, much of the very heart of the operation would go with it. Add to that its sheer inaccessibility, even if you used the old trail north from Cañada, which of course even now was not the wisest thing to do. Figure with that the poor intelligence about the place, once everything had gone berserk. And finally, of course, even linked to the question of its fate and precisely why it had met it, was that intangible factor about what else it had become: the mission of the golden boy, Father Andre Meinrad Mondragon.

Yes, the mission of Father Andre. Whatever that "mission" had been, in any sense.

You have to quit tormenting yourself with that question. Yes, Matthew thought resignedly, I do. If just to get this job done. I may not even know, when this adventure is over. I was his religious superior, and I have no idea what he was doing out here, what his "mission" was....

Though whatever answers might exist, they were to be seen shortly.

Felipe had come all the way back to Matthew, looking determined and sharp. He had toughened up and become nicely focused since they had gotten to know each other, Matthew saw. Any delay or refusal in getting to that point is another large goose egg in my record as a personnel manager, he mused. I won't even make the triple A league with seasons like this.

"Good, *bueno*." He waved Felipe back. Felipe had reported that they had reached the point where the path fully opened up, joining the old dirt road coming up from Cañada. They had passed more thatched dwellings, and at one point seen quite a lot of them. Toda had carefully questioned the residents and the news was the same. No soldiers, no men with guns for almost three years. But Matthew knew there were still patrols at large, with their own agendas, too. The new civilian government in Guatemala City teetered daily on the brink; few were helping, even knew how, much less had the resources. It was seen largely, even by its friends, as the creation of foreigners. Many, including the army, were said to be biding their time. For all hell to break loose again. Massacres had died out, but assassinations and targeting of certain persons remained common. And for sure, enough priests and religious had been targeted to have any illusions. But even if patrols were alerted, and even despite their mobility, Matthew still figured it would take practically five days for them to get here: one day at very least for the news to go out, on foot; over a day to get oriented and organized; three more at minimum to get in here. Okay, conservatively figure four. But we will be out of here by the end of the second.

In the widened mud road, big enough to drive a jeep or a small truck through, it all started to become familiar again. The way the sun broke through from the left side, from the west: it always seemed you had arrived here at the end of day. The dogs, domesticated animals and chickens, the pill-box thatched roof dwellings, brightly painted the way the natives loved them, even if now noticeably faded. The shoots of corn stalks and bean plants just outside the houses. But Matthew quickly saw that some of the dwellings were abandoned, dilapidated, paint chipped and fading, quickly being overtaken by

Casaroja

jungle again. And very few people, except old, wary women. One of the *communiqués* had said that many from the area had fled north, to Red Cross stations in Mexico, and Matthew believed it. That had been the way it was at about a dozen of the Casaroja outliers Matthew had ventured to; just an old sick man or woman left, too weak to travel.

Ravens flew over the grey patch of sky cracking out above the road, cackling and cawing, giant black scavengers. The path had still been kept clear enough to be a good hunting ground for them. There were some strong smells of cooking in the air, wafts of grey smoke rolling out of the bush. But there was very, very little visible human activity, at all.

Matthew patted his horse's strong neck. The beast had really performed splendidly. He did little enough riding himself anymore; Brother Miguel maintained this animal which he called Sebastian. Matthew appreciated a good working animal and treated them well, but was not sentimental about them. He rarely talked to them by name but sometimes would mumble words at Sebastian to let him know everything was okay. Maybe I should just get over that, Matthew thought, this horse at present is very critical to my well being. Maybe the beast would appreciate it and I might really start seeing something; maybe I have only been getting about 50% of him. Doubtless my animal management skills are as bad as my people management skills, I need to work on that. I need to work on many, many things.

It was only a few miles now. Matthew came to the place where there was a big bend to the right. He remembered that. Toda must already be at the village, he thought. Everything must be okay or I would have heard something, at least some noise or shouts. That Toda was a very, very fine man and Matthew had said heartfelt prayers in thanksgiving for having him. That Felipe was a crackerjack, too; certainly he would have made a ruckus if there was trouble. He is likely almost in there by now, too. They must be getting in there and checking it out carefully before nightfall; that is what they are doing. They are very good men and apprehend the entire situation. At a point like this, that little bit of jumpiness you see in Felipe is actually an asset, keeps him alert.

Here it came, the last great bend in the road, hard left. Straight west into Casaroja. It all came back as he went through it, just before it happened. Yes, yes: it had been a long time ago. But the road itself would expand into a plaza, that is how it was. Suddenly, there would be that opening of the road ahead, no longer a disappearing point smothered by foliage. And it started, just like that, again. Yes, they certainly must be in there, talking to the people.... They had to be; there was nothing else between Matthew and the village. He felt his heart racing up a bit.

Steady, he thought to himself. There is the opening. And here it comes when the buildings come plainly into view, growing from the center. He should be seeing red San Tomás Church with its little steeple. And the red painted activity hall right next to it, that Father Augustine had built immediately after. It was still plenty light, with the whole sky opening above, and he peered closer to see the buildings. Where were they? Where was anything? He wondered if his memory was playing tricks on him. No, certainly not. He remembered the last houses before the plaza and there they were. Now the forest fell all back, as he remembered well. He looked closer as he rode straight on in, to see....

Nothing.

Nothing...but a crumbling pile of brick, a wide cleared out area...maybe half a wall of one corner of the church, a fraction of the steeple.... The whole village looked abandoned. Except there, yes, Toda and his burro at the far end. And Felipe and his burro just across the way. Felipe waved: all was well. Both were talking to small groups of women and children. Virtually all the houses deserted, some also destroyed. He continued leading his horse, straight across what once had been the black and white tile floor of the church hall, now crumbling away. Yes, where that terrible picture had been taken. And he rode over that, and then straight across the remains of the black and white tile floor of the church itself. The same tile pattern as the kitchen at old Saint Benedict's Abbey...as the ground floor at Saint Maur's.... Father Matthew dismounted, patted the horse.

"Good boy, Sebastian," he said soothingly. A good enough moment in your life to start talking to animals by name, he thought. It was no more unreal than what they had come upon, here.

Casaroja

This was all that was left of Casaroja.

There was little to even say about it, Matthew saw, as the entire devastated impression sunk in, the astonishing, bitter end to this long journey. There was evidence, however, and one could still smell it: ashes, death. This great leveled bowl, where once a village had been, was the product of an absolute fury. Bricks still lay where they had fallen, scattered some distance away, and charred pieces of roofing and foundation. There were big piles of dirt just beyond the outline of the church, and some odd filled holes inside. Some were decorated, Matthew saw when he looked closer, with little crosses and ribbons, gifts. Graves, he recognized. There were some mounds farther off too where other structures had once been. There was the charred remnant of their former radio tower, just a few rusted, rootlike shreds of tubular steel twisting from the ground. All in all the place had been totally scoured out, and still cried out in a great collective voice of horror. Rather than even try to rebuild, the simple but sound instinct of the survivors had been simply to avoid the place. It was gone. It was over.

So nothing but a crime scene remained, Matthew mused. And an old one. Need not have worried much about that, he realized, but it also made him shiver a bit. An appetite this ravenous was not going to return here soon, for the mere scraps that remained. But of course, beyond that dimension, something more remained, too. One felt that oppressively. Matthew immediately went to his pack, pulled out his large crucifix and draped it around his neck, fixing the corpus plainly center on his shirt. There was going to be much work here in the next two days.

Felipe was walking over, wearing a face understandably somewhat stunned. He and Toda had already gleaned the basics. There was nothing else here, except what they had already seen. Those left from the village had scattered beyond the old plaza, though there was a larger grouping about seven miles northwest, a small settlement. Toda was going to go up there shortly. Almost all the men were dead, and many women, Toda had been told upon arrival. Some men had settled into the new little village from other areas. Soldiers had done it, a big group of them, probably a regiment. They had camped out in the church and hall and around them; corpses were buried beneath their floors and many, many just outside here. A very big *escuadrón de la muerte*. This was all some years ago, probably early 1983. The whole place had been made a *matadero*, a slaughterhouse; people had been taken into the church buildings and never seen again. About before that time, what led up to it or caused it, no information at all yet. The *indígena* just considered the place bad luck. It was a graveyard, that was all.

"No," Father Matthew gently cautioned Felipe, "Esto será cementerio, tierra consagrada."

"Sí." He looked a little perplexed but was nodding.

Matthew picked up a stick from the ruins. He walked over past the upraised mounds of dirt off the surviving corner of the church, apparently a mass grave. He walked off an area five times that size, scratching in the earth with the stick, a big square. There, he instructed Felipe, this will be the cemetery, I will bless the ground: we will lay out the bodies from this grave, bring in the dead from any other graves, and properly rebury them here.

"Desenterrar…." Felipe's voice trembled a bit as he contemplated Father Matthew's words.

"Yes, Felipe. This is the completion of the penance I told you about, under the waterfall, remember? And yes, it is truly very grim work, *labor espantoso*. But afterwards you will feel fresh as rain. As well you should. But go tell Toda I need at least seven men. More if we can get them. Tell them to bring shovels and hoes and rakes. Picks and axes if they can find them. They should still have many of those tools, somewhere. The people are very prudent and years ago we brought a truck full of these tools up here, brand new, and distributed them. I drove part of the way myself on the road from Cañada, Father Augustine and I in his International Scout, full of those shovels and farming implements…."

"Sí, Padre."

"And tell them to start early tomorrow, that the *padre* has come. Wake me up no later than five if I am not already up. Toda can sleep anywhere but you and I will separate and be off, somewhere, a little distance. I am sure it is all right here, but we have to keep up the same practices. Then in the morning you direct the work. Lay them out with dignity, Felipe, the best you can. Do not cover them yet. We will do that at the Mass, which I will say in the evening when the new graves are finished. Tell everybody that. And start writing down the names of all the dead you can learn about."

Matthew walked back to the remains of the church steeple. A fragment of red bricks about five feet high, the base of the little L shaped niche from which the bell once hung. "I will sit out here parts of the day tomorrow," Matthew said, "whenever they want me, to baptize babies and hear confessions. Let Toda tell them that if there are any marriages that need to be blessed, the couples should come here too. Then we will straighten this place up, then the Mass and then we refill the graves and bless the earth. And then I will replant the cross of Jesus Christ here. Do you understand all that?"

"Bueno, sí, Padre."

"Can you and Toda get all that across?"

"Sí, Padre Matthew."

"Good. And then you and I and Toda will get out of here, Felipe, day after next. Again, this is a precaution but we still cannot be too careful. We have no idea who these new people in the new village are. They are probably okay, but we do not know them. Or some innocent man or woman might be heading out of here on some road, get waylaid. Who knows? Or a friend of a friend, or a relative. The people who did this have no interest in this place anymore, but believe me, they do not want word to get out, either. They do not want to be identified, and there are still people here who might someday identify them. There are those who want them brought to justice, understand? You may have heard about that—it has started, the accounting for *la violencia*. Some of the best known sites of massacres have already been unearthed. Understand? This one too has long been rumored in this country by word of mouth. So even though there is no problem now, word of our being here could quickly start trouble…."

"Sí, está entendido."

"*Bueno*. Yes. So afterwards I will go back the way we came in. I am sure I can find it, I have it memorized. And then you and Toda get out of here quickly as you can, taking the old way. Follow the trail to Cañada but keep a big distance beyond it, not right on it, understand?"

Felipe looked as if he wanted to protest, was getting choked up a little. "Padre..." he began.

"See to it just like I told you," Matthew cut him off, "And come see me this summer at my monastery. I will give you instructions when we leave here, understand?"

"Sí, Padre Matthew."

It had gotten quite dark, though you could still see the outlines and shapes of things. It was very quiet except for some birds squawking in the distance. Here came Toda, walking over across the desiccated space with a small group of people. As they came up Matthew could discern three old women and a young man. Toda's face had settled into an impenetrable mask of silent witness, beyond sadness or any emotion. He had quite obviously heard a lot already, more than could even be articulated.

"Padre...." The women used the formal Spanish, gave a slight bow, and Father Matthew blessed each of them. The last, the elder of the group, embraced him in a markedly formal manner.

"María Bon," Matthew heard himself saying, recollection flooding him. He remembered it all, years ago up here with Father Augustine, all the days. This woman had been with them for decades, the center of their community. She had learned Spanish in her childhood and well, when her parents worked on a plantation. Yes, that was the keen face, the stark profile of hair setting off the face, ravaged now but green eyes still holding you, glinting. And this other was her cousin, the other María, the demure one. He did not recall the third woman. The young man was hardly a teen, would have been a child when the horrors passed through. It was obvious he only dimly knew what a priest was, this rather slender and pale youth. But he followed the women and remarkably imitated their gestures. Matthew placed his hand on the young man's bowed head, slowly pronounced a blessing.

María Bon succinctly told Matthew the story in Spanish. They came right in and went for the church. A dozen of them. Some people ran away, right at the beginning, but most did not. They were soldiers, and they mounted their guns and walked around in boots, set up a camp. They took their time. They got comfortable. Then after a few days they announced there were some men they were looking for. One by one they started taking men into the hall. Screams and cries were heard; the men were not seen at all again. Two of her own sons were lost. Then some women were raped, others taken in. After two weeks the whole squad appeared, surrounded the village, and "everybody died; everything was destroyed and burned all at once…."

"Enough," Matthew raised his hand. She was not crying but she was shaking. In the dying light she was still looking at you that way, too, a fire in her eyes, the old fire that Matthew still remembered. Augustine had cultivated her as their mission's "key man" under their old tried and true way of doing things, deducing in this complicated remote village that it was best for them to use this woman. And there was something else in her eyes too, a fire of another kind. She was fixed that way, the rest of her life, he saw. They were all fixed from that day forward, in whatever way they were then, and that was the way they were each going to be for good. God knows how they survived or what all their individual tales were; it did not matter. You would open the subject there with them only if they wanted that. You had the other questions but they would have to wait.

Matthew thanked the women, gravely and formally, bowing toward the little party with deep respect. He grasped María Bon's hand, assuring her they would talk more tomorrow. He saw a suppressed but discernible shudder pass over her. But only if she *wished*, he quickly added.

"Bueno Padre, bueno…."

They faded away.

"So what about the priest," Father Matthew turned to Felipe, "did Toda learn anything?"

Felipe slightly shook his head, "Disappeared too. The women could only say, 'with the rest.' This group does not seem to have precise information, Padre. It seems he was not seen from the very beginning. But perhaps some others would know better. She suggested that."

Matthew waved it off. He was vastly tired, and there was all the work ahead. They would do and learn what they could. They would have to be satisfied with that. Already however it was obvious that what he would glean here was going to be unsatisfactory. They had come in and gone right *for the church*.... María Bon's eyes had lit up at precisely that point. And had been looking right and hard at me, Matthew recalled, *as if I knew something.* She would not spell it out, however, no. And she stayed vague too: the soldiers were looking for "some men"—but who exactly? She did not name them. But did not say she did *not* know, either.

Perhaps all this was only a remnant of a general and wise fear in this village. But there also seemed, at bottom, a disturbing angle—a variation on other massacre stories Matthew had heard over these years. Yes, and running straight to my priest, Matthew rued. Well, when we find him we may learn something. Otherwise? There really was not much time, though it underscored his own caution in having opted for a short visit to *this* particular mission station, for the time being. Unlike the others...but he had inarticulably sensed that about the Casaroja black-out for a long time. The enormity of this tragedy, in many dimensions, was only now starting to hit him, on an emotional level. That slender, shaky, but fine remnant of steely resilience in the old leader, María Bon, had shaken him deeply too, to the root. Dear precious, gentle Lord, the seeds You plant....

But suddenly, as he was preparing to leave and make camp, shadows appeared against the last faint outlines of twilight. He could not make them out, just their forms as they appeared slowly, singly, two or three together at the most. Some carrying small lit candles, some wailing and weeping. Mostly, the very old, the survivors from nearby. They were starved for blessing; they could not wait. Father Matthew realized that it was going to be some time before he was allowed to sleep, this night. As darkness fell they kept steadily coming, to this vantage point he had established between the ruins, their shapes silhouetted against the night like a horde of ghosts.

THE DAY IN THE SUN

In the morning Matthew woke promptly after a sound dreamless sleep. The sky had completely cleared and it was very bright, the forest around the village loud with birds. Felipe was already off, but had carefully left him a pot of coffee on a circle of hot coals, and some fruit and bread that had doubtless been brought in by the women. Matthew ate, threw some water on his face, and dressed. It was going to be a very full day.

He left the little camp he and Felipe had carved out of the thicket late at night, emerged onto the plaza. Five native men, late middle-aged, were already seriously at work on the mass grave next to the ruin of the church. Stripped to the waist and with their pants legs rolled up, they somberly worked out the appalling dimensions of the grave from the moist red dirt. This grave was not too deep, only a few feet at most. Matthew walked clear of the edge, out of their way, close enough to see the way the skeletal remains lay upon each other in heaps, sometimes separated by remnants of clothing. He did not recognize any of these men but they had found those old shovels from decades past. They nodded grimly at him and he blessed them, and moved on.

In the full morning light he could survey much better the shape of the crime scene. More of the old black and white tile was left in the remains of San Tomás church, almost the full rectangle of it, though badly scorched and crushed. That, and some edges of the foundation no more than two bricks high, were all that even told you that this had once been a building. As to its function as a church, all traces had been completely erased. There was only that broken fragment of the little bell tower about four feet high. Just inside the corner of it, atop a few oddly untouched tiles, the people had endearingly set a chair for Matthew to use in performing his priestly duties today. It was just an old piece of office furniture of the type they still had down at San Plácido, from the early days, tubular steel framed and with red vinyl pads for the seat and back support. But they had saved it as if it were something special, and produced it now. It sat out there next to this fragment of the tower, the largest piece of anything left standing, in the center of 100 yards of wasteland in any direction, grave mounds and heaps of brick.

The community hall built by Father Augustine, informally known as Casaroja and from which the village had thereafter been known, was another story. Well over half the tile floor was gone, interspersed with these ugly dirt piles of graves. Are you waiting for me here, Father Mondragon? Matthew wondered. But for sure, there was not only no trace of the hall's function left, as a life center of Peter's barque, but from the extent of devastation you might not even know this had been *any* sort of structure at all, either. It did look like a fire had burned fiercely; large parts of the walls were lost in piles of ash and crumbled brick which followed no contours at all. Matthew tried to fix his memory of the place upon this heap, even using that terrible recollection of Salazar's photograph as an aid, but it was impossible.

Over the flat dirt plain of the lost village circled a growing flock of buzzards, flapping their wings. A few great hefty black ravens suddenly plopped out of the sky, right along the edge where the men were working. The men would shovel dirt in their direction to shoo them away, shout loud, pained curses. Intelligent, cool, and practically grinning, the ravens would simply hop back a few yards beyond the men's reach, waiting out this new and interesting activity.

Matthew ranged further, around the entire perimeter. There were a few of the old people still living where they always had, in homes of adobe or thatch. But not many; clearly the vast majority of these habitations were abandoned for good, the roofs and walls often collapsed. One long stretch of adobes had been systematically devastated, like the church buildings, knocked down and burnt.

Casaroja

As Matthew made his way back to the large grave, Felipe and Toda came walking across to him. Toda related that he had found another nine or ten men. The five at work had come over at dawn and these others were expected shortly. It appeared that there were two groups of brothers and cousins who had moved in about three years ago, and had taken wives from among the survivors. They were believed to be Catholic, perhaps attached to a Maryknoll mission three days' hike north beyond the hills. Many refugees had passed through there on the way out of the country. Very few men here had escaped with their lives at all, except for a few like the boy Juano they had met last night, protected by his grandparents who he cared for, in turn. Both his own parents had been killed.

As for the reason, Toda slowly shook his head, side to side. No, there was really no clue of that, beyond the usual accusations of soldiers that some of the village men had been revolutionaries. Had they been? Toda blinked at him as Felipe slowly translated Matthew's question. He answered carefully: the women said they did not know. Toda did believe that the women did not know or believe that. But he carefully repeated: they could not say. And as for the specific men the soldiers were looking for, the same answer from Toda: they could not say.

Or would not say, Matthew thought. Although he felt there had been no genuine revolutionary activity here. But Toda's report reinforced a feeling he had picked up since he first set foot here: that there was something critical they were holding back.

And of Father Andre? Toda did not blink, but momentarily turned his head away, looked at the earth. He raised his hand with a large rag, and wiped the sweat away from his brow under the line of his colorful bandana. He had been out working and digging already, himself. His look, Matthew mused, was almost one of shame in contemplating this question. But whether for his own professed Church, or for Matthew's missionary associate and for Matthew himself, as that man's superior, or even for the hopelessness of Toda's own people's plight into which that *ladino* had fallen, it was impossible to say. Perhaps, Toda was ashamed for all of it. It was as if Toda had fallen into a little reverie, brief but fathomless. Matthew had seen the look before in this *indígena*, once or twice.

Then Toda was back, in the here and now. His green eyes were looking calmly into Matthew's own.

"Camenak," Toda stated clearly.

Felipe flashed Matthew a quick, sad, sidelong glance. "Está muerto," Felipe translated softly, but Matthew had understood.

"Where? Why?" Matthew asked, determinedly.

"Nobody knows," Felipe said, "Nobody we talked to."

"Somebody knows," Matthew stated, decisively. Well, that was a hunch anyway, probably a good one, but no more. But do not let these people doubt your resolve. "Keep working on it," Matthew said to them, "and have Toda talk to the women more closely, if that becomes possible. I do not want to press these poor women myself. I have priestly work to accomplish, you understand. But I am quite sure that María Bon at least has some suspicions."

"Maybe we'll find him under the red house," Felipe offered.

"That's the least of my problems," Matthew ventured, for the first time being fully candid with this, his new *compañero*, for better or for worse. I did not want to have to get to this point with this man, he thought, but we have only a short time here. "I want to know what in hell *was going on with my priest*," Matthew raised his voice and laid it out as bluntly as he could, some of the emotion for once bursting out of him, "what if anything his...*actions*...had to do with what happened here—with *anything* that happened—understood?" It sounded lovely in Spanish, Matthew thought. Even Toda's big bat ears were picking up the music. And Felipe had registered not only the music, but also its import, Matthew immediately saw. Well fine, the priest figured, I finally said it.

"Acción, sí."

"Sin operación," Matthew emphasized.

Felipe' lip curled silently; he gulped. He was starting to get the picture even better. But suddenly it was painful, once again, to look into this poor fellow's face, so much like Andre's.

"And his *words*," Matthew sang it out suddenly and bitterly, with mocking inflection, "and his *teachings*, his *vocabulary*. I want to hear all about that, as much as they will tell you, understood?"

"Está entendido."

"*Bueno*. Yes. And was he *gentuza*? And if so, what kind of riff-raff was he? You see, dear friend, I do not know. Was he just a *bobo*? Or something more, see? A *revolucionario*? Or a friend of *la revolución*? Or, who knows, a *desatinado*, a blunderbuss?"

Matthew just stood there, arms folded, in the midst of this horrendous shipwreck. But Felipe had registered it all. Felipe was shaken; he had been shaken to start with. But he saw for once, the whole picture, the innermost part of this adventure he had signed on to. Maybe for once he understood the caution, the secretiveness.

"Do not press the women too hard," Matthew finally cautioned, "just do what you can. Maybe it's impossible…."

Matthew slapped Felipe on the back, then strode off to pray his office. And to pray, too, for the grace to keep his emotions more securely in control.

And for once, dimly, the truth began to penetrate his soul: *he's gone….*

*   *   *

The work on the graves had been going very well. The large grave alongside of Casaroja hall had been completely exposed to its bottom and all corners, and now they were carefully releasing the bodies from it, one by one, and laying them out straight. Felipe informed Father Matthew that this grave contained over a dozen. At one point, they had been so heaped on top of each other, that separation and identification was more difficult. A row of clean, gold brown skulls, stained the same color as the earth, had been neatly laid out along the rim of the trench.

The rest of the men had come down from the north and other graves were being searched out. There were plenty at work and it began to move faster. Those heaps inside the church and hall proved to have no more than two or three bodies each, limbs usually bound, limbs sometimes hacked off. Most of the dead had some identifying clothes. With the females many retained ringlets of black, braided hair. In any event the villagers seemed to have little problem identifying virtually all of them. Felipe dutifully walked along with Matthew's lined ledger book open, carefully recording the names, ages, and other information regarding the dead in dark blue ink—

Michael Morow

Mateo Paiz	29	father
Isabela Paiz	27	wife, mother
Lucas Chuc	44	father
Diego Chuc	61	grandfather
María Chuc	13	daughter
Victor Peñasco	24	husband....

 Suddenly there was a great deal of activity upon the plaza. Natives had gradually been making their way in all day, including whole families. The women openly mourned, wailed and cried over the bones as they were cleared and arranged, placing little candles at their heads or inside their rib cages. The row of skulls along the rim lengthened; large flowers had been fastened atop each of them, red and blue and yellow. More men came and pitched in. Silently and lithely, all in harmony like a great machine, they steadily rolled the earth back across the whole pit like a carpet. Wheel-barrows were produced to remove large piles of dirt, per Matthew's instructions that the new graves be dug deeper. No wholly intact mummies were found, and, thankfully, few heads carrying enough remnant of flesh to display fixed, final grimaces of pain. The earth had done its work well in these years and the bones were quite clean. But of course that old familiar smell was there. Nor did the black buzzards fail to notice the work—vast waves of them now circled more precariously above, and some were appearing in nearby tree tops.

 As the skeletons were reverently laid out in rows facing east, a little old man in clean shirt and pants appeared. He carefully hovered over each one with a small straw brush, dusting away any residual dirt, leaving them clean and dry.

 Matthew pulled out his first little disposable camera and quickly used up about half of the shots. Here's to you, Salazar, *muchas gracias*, from Casaroja with love.

 But Father Andre had not yet been found. Felipe grimly shook his head as Matthew came up, anticipating the question. Andre had not been in one of the pits inside the hall where they had thought he would be. Nor could much beyond the generalities yet be gleaned from the women, which Felipe admitted was odd, given the number

Casaroja

of years he had been given to understand that priests had served here. Salida, the third old woman from the night before, had told Toda, Felipe reported, that no one really felt they knew this *padre*. It was entirely different from the old days with Father Augustine, they knew, but they apparently had gotten accustomed to it. Doubtless, it was because "he, like me, was of Spanish blood," Felipe offered, but Matthew shook that off.

"Well, we may never got to the bottom of it," Matthew said out loud, practically to himself. But it would be a relief if we could at least verify his bones, he thought to himself. What possibly had been going on here? Besides the obvious, that is, parts of which you already knew from other crime scenes, and from the grapevine... the paranoid, monstrous army, the cynical, callous revolutionaries, all as if playing out bloody scripts written far away, views of life as lunatic as spaghetti Westerns. Dear God.... Well, little time for such rumination.

Meantime, there were many practical things to be done. "Tell María Bon I need three large, clean bowls, Felipe," Matthew instructed, "and to have them filled with clean water and brought here. Next, get two men to remove two large planks from this rubble. Good pieces of the rafters if you can find them, not burned or damaged. One at least four meters and one about two. Carve the ends clean, and cut a notch across the large one about a meter down. Lash the short one securely across the notch in the shape of a cross. Make sure it is good and secure for all time. Then leave it lying against the wall here. How many dead have we tallied so far?"

"About eighteen, Padre."

"Okay. And we have hardly even started on the outlying graves."

"That is true."

"Well, make sure this new grave is widened out to the dimensions I showed you before, for a *cementerio*. That may still be big enough but we may not get the job all done today. We ought to leave by tomorrow night, anyway, just as we planned. Let them all know that, and also let them know to continue the project, and I will have a priest here within...."

Suddenly, Matthew's voice stopped. It was all fine when you were here, and active. But figuring the vagaries of San Plácido, and

God knows what else into the schedule, brought a vision of a brick wall. He knew it and felt it but could not articulate it. He was not a seer but there was some sort of problem, he knew.... *Well get on it, kid.* "Tell them a year," Matthew finally said, "and sooner if we can. But assure them we will bless all the dead and..." Same problem... *what was it?* The riddle of Andre? Something else? "...restore some sort of...*presence* here."

"Sí, Padre."

"Are there any to be married?"

"The ones from the north. The first ones here this morning."

"You mean they were not married at their Maryknoll mission?"

"They have little to do with that mission, Padre, in recent years, I am told."

Matthew just looked back into the *ladino's* face. Now that there was activity and direction he was cool and quite useful. His triangular head and deep features seemed more focused, and thus he reminded you less of Andre. And Felipe was learning fast, to impart exact information useful to Matthew's assessments. Wonderful for his learning curve but it left Matthew with questions about the larger picture up here that Felipe obviously could not answer. This about the Maryknolls was news of some kind, but Father Matthew would not have enough time to get to the bottom of it. If they were somehow spooked about that other mission, why even venture here? But whatever nonsense Father Andre Meinrad Mondragon had gotten into out in this wilderness, by intention or negligence, he had apparently not managed to completely kill the seeds planted here, for years, by Father Augustine. I felt good when I saw those new fellows this morning, Matthew thought. I must use some care and coolness in dealing with them. Thank you, thank you good Jesus, for their help and overcoming their fear.

"Very well. Tell them the third bowl of water is for them to wash their faces and arms with. Have the women produce some sponges and towels. Tell the men thank you very much for what you have been doing but there is something more important for you to do now. Tell them to put on shirts. I will be back in an hour to talk to them, then to perform weddings and the other sacraments. Felipe,

Casaroja

you are a very good man to have along on this mission, and your penance is proceeding very well."

The priest was already striding off again, back up the forest path to his camp site. All Felipe could do was stand there and watch, with a look, despite all the horror he had witnessed in these hours, of an even greater amazement.

*   *   *

Matthew had found a good lunch laid out as neatly as breakfast—fresh coffee on fresh coals, more bread and some *toto postes*, fresh greens, a large ripe pear, and even a bowl of turkey soup. In all the years he had been in this country, he had still never gotten over the well-ordered habits of these natives. And even here, after all these monstrous attempts to mongrelize them, all these hateful crimes, the people had, deep down, stood up to it. Dear Lord, Matthew prayed, thank you for this wonderful food and the opportunity to labor for these people. I cannot believe it, Lord, what fertile soil, the best that anyone could ever know, so why can I not get my confreres to understand? How have we lost so much; will we still lose more? Forgive me, Lord, for my own gross stupidity and incompetence, give me Your knowledge and power to remedy my own failings. And thank You for all this, through Your bounty, and in the name of Christ our Lord, Amen.

And as for Father Andre Meinrad Mondragon....

Well, better forget *that*, Padre, leave that one where it lies.... Matthew shuddered involuntarily all of a sudden, as if it were not 110 degrees in the shade but 50 below zero....

It was overwhelming, Matthew realized, it was overwhelming.... But no time for that, now. On with the drill.

The priest quickly finished his meal, washed his face. Then reached deep down in his saddle bag, located his white alb and pulled it over himself.

"Make me white, oh Lord, cleanse my heart..."

Where was the rest? He felt around deeper. There they were, the purple stole over the neck, the maniple over the arm....

"...that I may joyfully reap the reward of my labors. Restore to me, oh Lord, the state of immortality which I lost through the sins...."

Matthew finally threw on his pack with the rest of what he needed, and quickly headed back through the forest to the plaza.

On the red vinyl seat of his station stood a large black raven, clapping its beak. Ah, Matthew thought, the new *capitán!* Oh great Bishop, of the Diocese of Desolation, have you come to hear my report, or to deliver yours? And where is your ruby ring...on that claw perhaps? I stoop in homage....

Yeah it was pretty funny all right, until you saw that horrid morsel fixed in its mouth.... Bone dry as it all had looked this morning, this diligent fellow had found something. Matthew's gorge rising, suddenly and involuntarily he felt the whole suppressed undertow begin to overtake him, all his useless rage and tears. *And how many of your cousins have I blasted out of trees in my youth?* Matthew felt his soul turn; he almost remembered exactly how many, and many of the clinical details of his mindless executions, too...aggh, to just pick up that shovel over there, and....

Suddenly it was as if the sky blinked, for an instant beyond recall and in a brightness beyond all imagining. And carrying a warmth beyond any poor prayers you could even hope to send skyward. And in that light and warmth he blinked, too, and afterwards saw that no, after all, nothing had changed. Except that indeed the zesty raven was quite funny again, funnier than ever. And what did God, Who made it, care? Whether that was a fat insect in its mouth or somebody's little finger? For the bird was not black at all, it was blazed through with light and the glory of creation, doing well what it was properly created to do: eat, and eat well.

And maybe it was even one of Saint Meinrad's ravens, the hermit's doting and protective friends. It was tame enough, for sure. And the priest felt his heart crack as if a boy again, and all those wonderful crows he had shot were restored, and he was in his own woods again forever, and they with him. Oh good Saint Meinrad, Matthew prayed, through your intercession ask God to lead me, with the help of these your loving companion birds, to the fate of your namesake and our brother, my own wayward confrere Father Andre Meinrad Mondragon, through the Sacred Heart of Jesus and the Immaculate Heart of His Holy Mother Mary, Amen.

And the raven lit into the sky finally, sensing Matthew's approach, and a black companion nearby that Matthew had not seen....

He turned to watch them, and in the same instant saw María Bon pass nearby. She appeared headed from the widening mass grave back to her home, and she was walking very quickly. And she was with a companion, an old man Matthew had not seen, and she was hurriedly, furiously gesticulating to the fellow, loudly snapping at him in an endless tirade, obviously in full spate.... It was such an incredible sight, in itself, that it suspended the priest's wonder at what it was even all about. There was her marvelous bright *huipil*, a fine coin necklace catching the light, and those amazing silver streaks in her long black hair. She was simply showing off her best, making an example of herself for the rest of the village to follow.

There was a hoarse, low, guttural croaking in the sky punctuating its vastness: crruk...crruk-ccruk. Matthew looked up to see the two black ravens, flying off due southwest....

And when he looked down, he found the young men and women to be married already assembling. Here came four couples, each including one of the men from the early morning crew with their fifth, still a bachelor, standing aside with the braided rings. The brides presented themselves in a startling rainbow of hand-woven skirts, *huipils*, headdresses and ribbons. Three held tiny babies, and five other very small children huddled around the group. The men had diligently cleaned themselves up the best they could and had shirts on, and bright headbands and hats in the traditional style. Other family members grouped themselves behind, and beyond them stretched the blighted moonscape of Casaroja and the rest of the crew, still digging, and beyond that finally the great circle of green forest enclosing all this space.

Felipe had carefully set down all the names and the names of the children, then dutifully grouped them left to right in the same order in which they stood. He handed Father Matthew his ledger.

Matthew took each couple aside separately for several minutes, then gently questioned each individual separately, and counseled them, heard their confessions. They seemed to be at least essentially oriented, and understood the irregularity of their present situations. Apparently at a certain root level Catholic society had continued to function here, including a dose of moral teaching. They had some sincere doubt they would ever see a priest again, and he strove to resolve that doubt. He put them back into a group.

"In nomine Patris, et Filii, et Spiritus Sancti. Amen." Matthew blessed them, and began.

"Amen," they said as one.

"Domingo, will you take Catalina, here present, for your lawful wife, according to the rite of our Holy Mother the Church?"

"I will."

They proceeded through the ceremony, slowly and deliberately, each in turn stating consent, then each couple, joining right hands pledging each to the other, repeating the words after Matthew. Domingo to Catalina. Catalina to Domingo. Jorge and María. Reinaldo and Albina. Lazard and Alejandra, who finally concluded the vows in Kekchi.

"I, Alejandra Choc, take you, Lazard Tuye, for my lawful husband, to have and to hold, from this day forward, for better, for worse, for richer, for poorer, in sickness and in health, until death do us part."

"Ego conjungo vos in matrimonium," Father Matthew intoned, "in nomine Patris, et Fillii, et Spiritus Sancti...."

"Amen."

Matthew sprinkled them with holy water, and completed the prayers.

Tomás, the ring bearer, stepped forward and the braided rings were blessed in turn, and given to the couples.

"With this ring, I wed you, and I pledge you my faithfulness."

And blessing them again, Matthew led them through to the end, and gave them the final blessing.

"And a few words for you, now," Matthew said, and proceeded into an instruction of their marital duties, and of their duties to the Faith. "We came here many years ago," he concluded, "from southern Indiana in the United States, my monastery and base. Some of your parents may have told you of Padre Augustine. He is still with us, in another part of this country. I am in Cañada now, and am sorry I could not be here sooner. And I am sorry I have to leave so soon. You know why….

"I have still not found the priest who was here, Padre Andre. I am told he is gone with the rest, *camenak*. Let us never forget the horrors that have been unveiled here today, unveiled for our prayers in the same strange providence of God that brings me to join you, on the same day, in Holy Matrimony. I am astonished, humbled, devastated in the face of the faith of that remnant of this village, which brings you here today to exchange these awesome vows, in this terrible place. I find it so mighty and so pure, this astonishing power of faith, that I cannot even speak of it. Please excuse me. But I am telling you, we are coming back. After we bury the dead I am putting up the cross again, and soon we are coming back. I do not know how. I have to go back to my brothers for a time. We have to make sure there will be no more trouble for you on…our account. But we are going to do it. Please pray for me and my brothers at San Plácido in Cañada. Please bless us. Please bless each other, and these dead, and love each other, every day. You have no idea the power of your prayers. You have no idea the power of your love, the power of your blessing. Excuse me, I am speechless before it…."

Why did I say that, Matthew wondered, a little angry with himself. There was no saying it was *our* account, at least not verifiably. Well…. He braced himself. *No time for untruth anymore*, he rued.

It was time to baptize the babies. I am going to have to watch it, Matthew thought, I cannot even let myself start talking, cannot even let myself get off script. Telling them stupid things won't help them, either, if soldiers ever return.

María Bon appeared, as if on cue, thankfully. Resplendent in her own hand-woven rainbows, she produced the second big bowl of water. Already he felt as if all were in control, once more. Father Matthew duly salted the water, blessed it, mixed in a vial of blessed water all the way from Saint Benedict's Abbey in Indiana.

Little Anton was produced. His sponsor stepped forward. Matthew snapped back into his drill, clear and measured, deliberate.

"I baptize thee, Anton Chuc, in the name of the Father, and the Son, and the Holy Ghost. Amen."

And two Marías, a Jacinta, a Ruiz, a little Jorge....

And more followed these children of the married couples, some adults too. Matthew looked at his watch: ten till twelve. The word was they were still locating more graves. The Mass for the dead was not going to be today, he could already see; he still had confessions. He did not want to do a general absolution, even though there was ample justification. There was great, great spiritual healing that needed to occur here, a crushing amount, and at least some confessions had to be done individually. As many as possible. He could already feel that strongly. Well, he could certainly speed the baptisms up. He brought all the rest into the circle and had them say all the prayers together, blessed them with the water.

He waved them off and simply pointed to his red vinyl chair and went and positioned himself there, making the best effort he could to preserve some privacy for the penitents. María Bon helped by lining them up no closer than thirty yards away. The sun beating down on him strongly, Matthew bowed and said his preliminary prayers. Then, averting his face toward the remnant of red bricks, he put up a hand and motioned the first penitent over.

It went on a long time, over two full hours, even though he told each of them they need only relate their most serious matters. Given the circumstances, the hateful coercion that had been imposed here and the ensuing madness, how serious was any of it? Only God knew; certainly many of the sins here were mitigated. But there was certainly enough left over, oh yes, to fester and grow, wrench souls toward despair and coldness, and a host of other torments in all the time since. And so Matthew heard from a woman who had refused to speak to her husband for several days, she could not even recall why; then he was taken into the red house and never seen again. And from another woman, who slept with the soldiers in fear for her life. Indeed many of the survivors had corroborated with the killers in one way or another, or at least over time had convinced themselves that they had. So throw it all on the fire, Lord, burn it all away, forget it finally. Matthew found himself forgetting much of it almost instantly, as he prayed continuously through these stories, it was all so monstrous and overwhelming.

Finally, he drew the penitents together in a group and led them through some prayers, counseled and reassured them, finally dismissed them with a blessing. He watched them depart slowly across the sun-blasted plaza, amidst the business of the grave diggers. He went back to his chair, removed his vestments and packed them.

Pushing his accouterments down into the bottom of his saddle pack, he felt something, a small bottle. What was it? He reached for it and pulled it out. Whiskey? Packing seemed like a lifetime ago. He had entirely forgotten putting it in, this gift sent by his old friend Christopher, in thanks for those masks. There were some cigars, too.

Shielding his eyes, Father Matthew began to read this bottle:

BASIL HAYDEN'S
Kentucky Straight
Bourbon Whiskey

The bottle itself was a work of art, with a paper label draped over either side of the neck not unlike a Benedictine scapular, an iron band around its waist embossed with the bourbon's name, complete with a stylish buckle carrying the maker's initials. And its whole story: distilled since 1796 when both Kentucky and the nation were in their infancy, and George Washington President of the United States....

He began chuckling, then laughing. Against everything, despite everything, because of everything. Then he remembered himself, checked to see that no one was watching. The bottle had not been opened. I will deserve this if I can carry this adventure off, he considered. And then: well...it is not over yet but getting there.

He opened it and smelled it: straight as Kentucky. Aged eight years on hillside rackhouses, its story went on. He took a swig: fine. Nobody was looking; he took another. Wonderful. I am exhausted, he thought, I am as emotionally exhausted as I ever remember. He carefully tucked the gift back into his saddle pack. He slightly tipped his chair back against the remnant of the wall, and fell immediately to sleep.

* * *

When you closed your eyes, it was crimson, rosy, very bright... you knew... *I know*, Matthew thought, rationally, *I* know that I am asleep...and thinking it through, one step at a time. *Was I this tired? Am I this tired?*

Slow, slow circling shadows against the bright pinkish skies...but so tired that not even all this light can wake me. No, he thought, not that little taste of Christopher's whiskey...whatever it was. He could not think of the name, those shadows were more important. Buzzards? Ravens? It was quiet too, but a shout now and then pierced it...*voices*...near the—graves? He felt his face knit up in puzzlement. Why graves? Why indeed, he thought. We never had any trouble. We never had any trouble at all, all through those years of *la violencia*, as they called it. Never any trouble in Cañada—no real trouble, anyway. Not then and not now. Never. Or anywhere else, in all the missions and stations in this part of the country. Not all these years....

Yes, it had always been somewhere else, somewhere else. So what made it change, he wanted to ask the colored sky, why?

Crruk-crruk. Crruk-crruk-crruk....

The guttural call of a raven, right overhead, disappearing. A sort of answer?

He tried to look at it, tried to focus on this particular circling shadow against the crimson brightness. It was coming into view, too. Almost obediently. Come on, Matthew tried to order the mirage, deep from his sleep, come on!

And it started to obey, yes. See it? No raven, no. A sort of black wing spread, but strangely a human shape. See it clear and plainly, he ordered his own vision, again.

A second raven? No. Closer, closer: oh, yes. It made perfect sense. The figure of Jesus Christ, arms aggressively displayed, birdlike.... That woodcut, remember? How many times have you seen it, Father Matthew? More than a few, he recalled, trying hard to stay calm and rational. And what had you done about them, Father Matthew? Torn them down, he answered deliberately—trying to make his lips move, too, ordering them to move. You need to make this clear, he thought, very clear.

"I tore them down!" He spoke out loud, for a moment piercing the veil of sleep.

Crruk-crruk-crruk. Crruk....

Then the undertow of weariness took him, again, the old dream of a wave, a surf. But that image clear in his vision still—black and white....

No, *those* were not my neighbors, even then. Even before the worst years...I saw to that, too. I saw to it—no such blasphemous banners, even in town—I tore them down.

But he remembered them well, just as, occasionally, his memory could vividly reconstruct birds he had shot in his youth. Stark black and white, this bold travesty of the crucified body of Christ as if leapt down from the cross—the cross thrown to the ground behind. Defiant and wielding a whip over his head. Guns and torn pieces of money—clearly American dollar bills—at his feet with the ruin of a tank ablaze in the distance. A Christ aroused, enraged, a stark sign of holy vengeance.

"I ripped them down!" Matthew heard his own voice cry out of him.

But here came another dark, slowly circling shadow...another ravenlike shape. That *other* poster around town, remember? And as this one came into focus out of his memory it *was* truly a bird. *Remember?* Not a raven however, but a quetzal—a black and white woodcut of the national bird held up by an upraised hand. Surrounded in a circle by caricatures of corrupt pasty-faced politicians, dog-faced generals, points of swords and pointing American fighter jets aimed up at the bird in all directions. This had been the symbol of EGP, of course, the largest active organ of *la revuloción*. That poster had been an even rarer sight in Cañada, Matthew recalled.

But I did not tear *that* one down, no.... I did not like it, but that one was not *my* business.... Should it have been? No, he could only say. And there was nothing in his own training to tell him otherwise.

"I did everything I could." His lips moved...and his rational mind knew he was speaking out, in his sleep. "I did everything I should...."

To what purpose?

To keep these troubles away from our missions, from Jesus Christ.... Did I fail?

Andre? Did I fail?

The red-faced mask of Ajitz flashed upon the now blackened background of his dream....

"What I could!" Somehow, his rational mind *knew* this was true too, despite everything. "I didn't send for him! *They* sent him to me!" he heard himself saying, to some others so deep in his dream he could not even see their masked faces.

And they did, didn't they? Oh brother. And what a send...that arrogant listlessness of his, passive aggression, languid insolence....

And how could you have forgotten what old Father Cuthbert Rendlemann tried to teach you? "Get them young and full of the enthusiasm of *boys*, ebullient! Yet sound and careful, and as vigorously strong as men in their prime years!" Quite the *exact opposite* of our dear missing confrere, would you not say, Father Matthew?

"He was *sent*! *I* didn't ask for him!"

Cruk! Crrruk!

Are you laughing at me then, birds? Well I did everything, everything....

Or did you?

Father Matthew thought about it, slowly, like the gliding shadows.... Was there *something else*? Something I did myself, perhaps even unwittingly? He scanned his memory, imperiously rejecting a dozen self-rebukes. No, no, no, no, no....

And then...*eh*, a sick and sinking feeling. *That*? It could not have been, he protested.... But then, what else??

Another dark shape seemed to pass between his gaze and the sun...and Father Matthew tried to make it out....

You remember how it is with priest-revolutionaries, a voice from nowhere spoke to him....

"Sure I do. How could I help that?" They were here in this country...those others....

"It's a coded message from Archabbot Kreidler." It was Brother Peter's voice, clearly, back at San Plácido. "To you," Brother Peter continued, "It seems that Father Stephen Durković is going to be coming up here in a few days...some sort of 'fact-finding' tour of the whole country...."

Matthew just glared at him, instantly enraged. Said nothing, just silently raged more....

"Go on," Prior Matthew eventually said.

"I believe the archabbot would like you to show Father Durković around the house, let yourself be interviewed.... Well, I think you should read it closely for yourself...."

"Of course."

"He does mention, ah, your *considered* discretion...."

"Of course." Matthew frowned, looked away, at the walls. He brooded. Yes, for sure, you know how it is with priest-revolutionaries. You have known a long time. They intrigued you so much when you were a kid, remember? All the way back to your minor seminary days...reading about them in books out West that summer at Saint Maur in the Dakotas. But those priest-revolutionaries you only knew in books. However stupid and skewed, your youthful romanticism about those priests was years before you actually had met one yourself. You had to come to this country hoping to do that, of course.... But dear Lord, get this guy out of here. What is Abbot Kreidler even thinking? What with unprecedented upheaval and rumors of massacres....

"By the way, Peter," Prior Matthew eventually said, "our good Brother David has not seen this message, has he?"

"Certainly not. Your instructions have been followed to the letter. New codes constantly. And this message from Abbot Kreidler just came in by ordinary mail, and it came to me. I decoded it personally on the new program David has stored on the computer."

"Excellent work, Brother Peter," Matthew tried to sound calm, "Well, I guess you better show it to me."

They marched into the office, darkened against the mid-day glare, Matthew leading the way in an almost military stride. Even uncoded, the letter was precisely as naive and blandly nonsensical as Matthew expected. Kreidler was a pawn, all right. Of Wildenmut, at least. But of who else? Matthew had tried to keep a lid on this "coded messages" business, yet still wondered who else had already, or could have, access to that message. Durković coming was bad enough.... But at least the day had not yet arrived that the Pig rhapsodized about, when "computers will talk to each other." Or had it? The prior realized he did not even know.

All right, he thought, battle stations. Brother Pig's machine was turned off, Matthew could see, the dull green screen staring as blankly as a moon man's visor. Maybe we have not been careful enough, it occurred to him then, letting Brother Pig play with this toy. Especially right now. For there were no jokes in this country, anymore.... Who else around here might know how to play with this thing? Only David and Peter as far as he knew. But anybody could turn on a machine...and who else had access at or via "the Hill"? This silly psalmic jargon David and Peter had devised for radio talk was bad enough, but there was nothing to be done about it. And at least that was strictly in-house—but who could say about this other? Matthew realized what he had to do: remove any physical evidence of this "code" coming in from the States for the time being. He paused near the entrance to the room, thinking about how exactly to disable the computer.

His first instinct was just to smash it, knock it off the desk as if by accident. But who knows, he thought, that might not even be effective. Nor did he want to start a legend going in the house about his own wacky behavior. Okay, he figured, Peter is trustworthy, just face the issue. To a point....

"Peter," Matthew stated plainly, "just memorize the codes from now on, okay? Then get this stupid computer out of here, and lock it up deep in the cellar, got that?" He pulled his keys out of his pocket and handed them over.

"Ah...yes, Father Prior." Peter was being formal, puzzled that Matthew had uncharacteristically given a directive without a reason. Well, I don't care to state my reason, Matthew fumed a little to himself. But I better tell him something.

"I'm not sure how secure the archabbey's *messaging system* is, either, you see...." Better than saying anything about the archabbot himself not being very secure, Matthew figured.

"Yes..." Brother Peter had droned on once more. What the devil are you doing, Matthew wondered, bucking for sub-prior? "But you know," Peter irritatingly continued, "we might be able to figure that out and check their codes here, Brother David is very skilled—"

Casaroja

"He's not to know!" Matthew tried to avoid thundering it out, or casting an aspersion on the Pig. "This is *sensitive*, Peter, damnit!" He saw that well-known face on Peter, of a stunned rabbit before his superior. And when are you going to learn to control yourself, the still-green prior had chastised himself, your fresh tongue is the least of it. "Look—I'm sorry. Just get it all out of here right this minute, and don't tell anyone, you hear?"

A quite flustered but dutiful Peter was already yanking out wires, putting the preposterous contraption on a roll cart and heading for the exit.

"Excellent, Brother Peter," Matthew called after him, in a determinedly cheerier tone, "I'll let you know one night when we can sneak it back in...."

"David will be very upset...."

"Who cares!!"

The door swung shut—good riddance!

Well, that fixed that.... No weird messages about, now, coded or un-coded, for sure, and none of the Pig's handiwork as he punches them out on a greygreen screen, afterwards available to who knows who?

The next evening, Matthew stood back inside the entrance courtyard and took in a deep impression of his unwelcome guest, the one and only Father Stephen Durković. Matthew had been occupied and had missed the essence of it at first, he was realizing, and just found the man's aura distracting and irritating. But finally he beheld it plain as day. It was that worn look of an old revolutionary. Yes, you have seen them, yes. Matthew had by then even come to recognize it, and by then also in priest-revolutionaries. That had been a jolt at first: that same colossal weariness oddly conjoined to a canny alertness, simultaneously. Alertness not to the sort of things which alerted yourself, either, but alertness to their opposites. Most likely he was looking at you in that sick way too. So there was this simple rudeness on one level, the veteran revolutionary treating you and whatever else as something of no interest, like a thing. One's natural reaction to such insult, however, was strong enough to trigger in a Christian an automatic self-rebuke, an over-compensation. That reaction,

Matthew had come to see, next diverted the object of such indifference from a deeper, more dire observation. Of an absolute depravity. The realization of being in the presence of such a corrupt spirit, animating a fellow priest, was quite overwhelming and shattering. You never really got over it.

Perhaps they had cynically figured on that though, too, Matthew coolly ruminated. They were that subtle, studied and practiced. They had a terrible worldly wisdom, plus the advantage of an entirely integrated and whole world view that explained everything, made action easy. They had everything we on the other side had, in the good old days, except Christ. Burdened by Christ, as they well understood, pangs of conscience and doubt would never allow us to see things with the same clarity, particularly about them, much less allow us to hang our actions upon such chimeras of human interaction. Indeed, Matthew had come to see, this deliberately rude initial stance of the *revolucionario*—of superiority, indifference, and disdain—could never be abandoned by them, nor Christ entertained at all. Then it would all go to pieces. Yes, they could try to con you about Jesus and the Church, lay in plenty of words from the bible too—often they were quite loud about all that really—but they could never genuinely go there. And being Christian you, in turn, could never go finally to judgment upon them, and you often enough stopped far short even of full observation. They also counted on that. And the effect often held you at precisely that point, too, forever a moth hovering above a transfixing, hypnotizing flame.

How had I even first come to see it myself, Matthew wondered. He could not recall, it had been awhile. Must have been by accident. Caught it all out the side of an eye when one of these jokers was not looking. There were many moments like that, truth be told, because though they spoke much of dialoguing, listening, seeing, hearing, in truth they saw only what they came to see. They talked like parrots, ground all the world's variety and splendid contradiction down to the same stereotyped lens: haves, have nots, powerful, powerless. Nothing else: no other dimension admitted or allowed. Yet they so monopolized your attention, as always, that you could not help watching them, close up especially. And Matthew was even starting to think there was a certain definite smell to all of them. Quite indescribable because, matching the sheer incredibleness of their being, it was not of this world. Though hardly of heaven, either.

Well, Matthew figured, the two of us have come a long way from home to have this stand off. On with it.

So here he came, finally, "Little Skeed" Durković, Christopher Gauthier's old pal. Making the rounds, probably hard at work on another incoherent poetic anthem to himself, disguised as an inside look at Central America. He had come into town with much fanfare and amongst all the usual suspects, plus a few new ones including a videocam fellow. This was bad news for the prior of San Plácido, who was trying to lie low in these dangerous years of civil war gone mad. Matthew had been watching the celebrity priest for some time, as the Skeed studiously avoided introducing himself, chatting constantly, constantly in some sort of nervous fit to his stone dumb entourage of sycophants, who were hanging on his every nervous gesture and cascading intonation of sounds. It was basically in English, mixed with a stew of Hispanic slang, mispronounced Kekchi, and old Church Latinisms—the last apparently for laughs. But what could it matter.... The only consistent note in it was straight southside Chicago cloutspeak, nasal chops of stage directions for his traveling Apocalypse show.

Yes, in old Skeed's fevered imagination doubtless there existed already all the bombs, gunshots, stabbings, assassinations, explosions necessary for a whole world war. He had so obviously come to Guatemala with a consuming hunger for such experiences that he was ready to explode all by himself, with the drop of a hat. Matthew had already observed one such occurrence. When they had all been chatting out there in the courtyard, an old car had apparently come up the path and its smoking engine popped. Father Durković had all but hit the decks, his eyes and nose flaring dramatically, while simultaneously his entire tiny figure arched itself into a posture of high holy rage and righteous indignation, ready to call down the wrath of God on this murderous assault. When he realized what it was finally, the Skeed just as visibly sagged. Like a wilting plant, though not without a lingering air of disappointment behind his thick glasses—yes, even of hurt.

I am going to have to brave it, Prior Matthew told himself reliving it now, in his slumber, *and I am going to have to swallow my pride too*. Fine! Well though...I *did* it. How did it go again? One step at a time, he recalled. And the first step was simply to *disarm* the man... deprive him of his intrusive, accursed machine, his dear precious videocam. But had I done that? The fact that this berserko came here must *never* be verified....

Probably I should just have had Brother Pig deal with him, Matthew thought. Whatever else he was, the Pig was brawny. And that was muscle in his arms too. I should just have had the Pig throw him off the property. Why, again, such hesitation? And the Pig would have happily done it too, for that was one thing about him. He had at least one of Saint Benedict's prime monastic virtues—prompt obedience. Well, maybe one or two others, if you allowed yourself to admit it. He had that old boyish ebullience and enthusiasm that the old mission hands prized, for sure.

But I had not used him. No. The prior could only remember too well his own solution....

"Well, come now, Father Steve, it's been too long and we've not even properly met yet..." And so with that Matthew had simply marched into the little circle of hangers-on, and swept up "the Skeed" as Christopher so fondly called him—blue denim Maoist beret, peace medallion in place of a cross, well-faded Che Guevara get-up and all—straight back into the San Plácido enclosure and into the privacy of his office. Away from them all, and especially away from all accursed sound recording and image recording devices.

It had actually embarrassed Matthew how effusively and warmly the little fellow then responded in kind, making the prior feel that he had perhaps been too condemnatory about the Skeed, from a distance. Father Steve's eyes positively glowed; he seemed unable to complete a sentence in the face of Matthew's expansive personality and easy intimacy. So it was all fun for a time as they talked about what great things each had heard about the other from their mutual friend Christopher, and also about certain fundamental things concerning this country Guatemala and their Church here, upon which they could not help but to agree. As for this last litany, it struck Matthew as perhaps a little too quick, a little too long, a

Casaroja

little too obviously premeditated. Likely even rehearsed. The prior kept his guard up.

"Ah, in times like this," Father Steve eventually gestured animatedly, "it seems truth can hardly be told except badly—too much emotion! Without context, with too much information both unknown and shocking to the outside world...."

"Sure," Matthew heard himself stating dryly but earnestly—for perhaps the tenth time already, he realized. But his guest seemed not to mind.

"But in that regard I'd say prophesy is the only vocabulary we have left." The little priest continued, "And in that I'd certainly be the first to say that your own *History of a Benedictine Foundation in Peru* remains even to this day a sheer marvel, a—"

"Thank you very much," Matthew heard himself saying, quickly cutting off the canned flattery, "You're too kind." And too darned sleazy, he also then clearly thought, for once. But I guess I laid myself too wide open to avoid that one.

"When I first visited *this* country years ago," Father Steve went on undeterred, "Christopher had just sent me a copy of your thesis. And as we went to each village your words made everything new, as if I were seeing everything on the first day of creation. Everything you wrote about Peru only doubly applied in Guatemala."

"Well, I guess, fortunes have changed," Matthew put in without emotion.

"Prescient, Father, very prescient," the Skeed took him up on it, a cast of seriousness falling over his face. Matthew noticed it; how strange, he thought, how quickly his face changes yet again. Fast as one of those blinking multicolor Christmas trees the natives so loved here, this must at very least be the hundredth face I have seen on this fellow today.

"Just experience, I guess," Matthew continued his play of terse self-effacement, his own sort of verbal con game he well knew. And likely, just then, a tactical error with a man of this sort, his instincts later told him. "But no experience is really necessary to see how fortunes have changed here," he tried to clarify, and also to back off.

"The secretest parts of fortune," the celebrity revolutionary said with a sort of hushed seriousness, "*as* they say."

Michael Morow

I shouldn't have sat down at the gambling table with one of these literary criterary bozos, Matthew scolded himself, I'm out of my league. Leave them to the likes of Christopher. But the prior decided to up the ante anyway, he was getting tired of this game. "Maybe the news you are getting is not *true*, Father," Matthew said slowly and directly as he could, "Let me state this more plainly. Because what is contributing to the disasters here is not particularly secret. Parts of it betray a certain *intentionality*, so we *should* say. If we want to be honest, that is. For thinking or *saying* or *reporting*, if you get my message, does not change the essence of a thing. But it can greatly affect how the story about it goes out into the world and grows.… So let me just ask you, Father Durković, what brings you smack to the very middle of this doomsday land? But no, let me guess…your reputation precedes you. Do you just have a very private taste, my good friend, for this so very particular and unique patch of Armageddon?"

Little Skeed faded a little at that, for a clear second or two. And then flashed a bright toothed smile—obviously an instinctive defense mechanism. But then just as quickly drew back into himself, again. And made still *another* face, dear Lord, squinching up at you behind those pathetic glasses, curls of unkempt hair dangling down toward his eyes. But Matthew saw that he at least had finally made a hit, a palpable hit.

"You are very right of course to—"

"Of course I'm right." The prior of San Plácido pronounced each word slowly, meaning to settle the affair.

"Father—"

"Look," Matthew said grimly, hands clenched before him, "We both know what this is about…" Matthew considered, then rejected handing him the candor of Archabbot Kreidler's introduction. Doubtless this meddler already knew that, might even have a copy of it. No matter. "I just have a job to do here." It was banal, for sure, but it was the best Matthew felt he could do. It was an encompassing statement, and anyway it was true.

"We are big guys in this country, you know, Father Prior, even little guys like me!" Durković sort of winked a new face and a new mask. The public performer, Matthew figured, he has finally gotten down to his hollowed out essence.

Casaroja

"Christopher always said you were a funny fellow," Matthew winked back with a show of gaiety, a little sugar. He quickly saw that it worked, and felt the sugar turn sour inside him.

"We may like it or not," Father Durković launched ahead quickly, "and I am sure you *do not*, Prior Eberhard, you have a serious reputation and one of compassion—but we remain *americános*, you see. Whatever we do. And it is our country that is supplying the know-how to the army here, Reagan and his cronies and their phantasmagoria of blood, 'commies everywhere—root them out!' No matter how many of our innocent saints must pay. Those guns you certainly know, Father, straight from our lackeys in Israel. Using them to clean up the land—of *people*—make way for new dams, new roads, progress, the money men! *Father!* The peasant guerillas here aren't breaking any commandment! Our own Church—our theology teaches self-defense is justifiable as a last resort! And if *this* is not the last resort, what is? There are refugees in camps up and down this country and even *they* are being eliminated! Slaughtered! Father Prior, your pacifism is admirable but—"

"I'm no pacifist, thank you."

"But then...."

"What *can* I do? I'll tell you this, whatever I do or say will cause *no good*, will only cause more innocent people to die. You think this is America? You think 'speaking out' counts for something here?"

"A churchman of your stature needs say very little at all, Father Prior...."

"Oh, please."

But at this point all Matthew could do was allow the antic priest to continue his diatribe, lay the whole thing out. For one thing, however ludicrous and even offensive this Skeed character, it was hardly as if he spoke only untruth. But as it went on Matthew could only half listen. The pointed observations were all patched together by very old fudge. Have I not heard all this before, he wondered? The old argument, the oldest in the world. "I show you all this," as Satan said to Jesus in the desert, "all before you can be yours." The old appeal to pride and ambition, to what this world called heroic. That, obsessively buried in the most exaggerated virulent hate for America you could imagine; their country, never named but to defile it, was not merely stupid and reckless but the antichrist. Some subtle disdain for traditional missionary work too. A lot of words and some bad poetry, Matthew had mused, all Father Steve "the Skeed" Durković did was to give them Barabbas over and over to the point of nausea.

Dear Lord, how stupid can he think I am? Matthew wondered. Even if I agreed with his aims. But then Matthew felt somewhat reassured—obviously some of his own bad acting had worked on the fellow. Obviously the Skeed thinks I am only another sort of Chicagoland heavy, of that oafish strain marked by limited vocabulary and static stereotyped emotional responses. But he thought Christopher had once told him this guy had some background in parish work, of the tough inner city ghetto type. No, he figured, upon close live inspection, that was highly unlikely. There was precious little genuinely human here, not even that sort of rudimentary empathy which will rub off from such experience and exposure. The Mayans were just pawns, despite the Skeed's silly habit of calling them saints. They were only so much detritus, and they were being treated as such not only by this ungodly national army and a succession of puppet regimes, but also by the *indígenas'* own dubious spokesmen. He must be *mad*, Matthew marveled, absolutely loony. Father Steve Durković was so bad that he made the dreary jargon that came out of Andre's mouth look like Ivy league material.

"…just some *footage*, of your Mecca here, Father Prior…it reminds one of the old Jesuit utopias in Paraguay…the Gospel *come to life*, amidst ashes and bones…the beauty of faith shining through, implying the hope of justice…*a liberation of the spirit*…a phoenix? No, the Holy Spirit! Free! Above the cross, a canticle never annulled, unrestrained and unrestrainable, challenging the heights! The mad saga set aside! The dialectic of competing brute behemoths, crushing all under foot—all of that transcended! An image will say a thousand words—you need say *nothing*, sign nothing…."

How stupid he must *certainly* think I am, Matthew considered again, to fall for this one. How would they edit even the most innocent of footage? What will *their narrator* say, over silent images filmed here? Matthew was about ready to call Brother Pig, to physically throw both the Skeed and his camera man off the premises and to stomp into dust any footage they might have already covertly made....

He turned in his sleep...*did I do that?* In his deep slumber he could not remember...did I get Brother Pig to destroy the footage? Did they run some propaganda with images of me? Oh merciful God... has my negligence brought this evil to Casaroja?

But he could not fathom it, only tossed restlessly more....

And saw more shadows pass beneath the sun....

The strange big city rasp of Stephen Durković's voice....

The terrible uncertainty that his visit had somehow linked the mission house to *la revolución*, ending in this devastation....

Like a swimmer deep in murk, Father Matthew dove for the answer, deeper yet, only to find himself more assailed by self-accusation, his head burning in a thousand places....

* * *

Abruptly, Father Matthew sat up, realized he was awake.

It was late in the day, he saw. Long shadows stretched across the plaza where men still vigorously worked. He had a splitting headache. His mind and consciousness were overwhelmed, he now knew. Sleep had helped him little...he could only imagine how exhausted he had been. He saw that someone had lovingly put a blanket over him, as he had tilted back against the remaining scrap of wall in that red chair....

Andre, I am sorry....

He stood up, wiped off his face. The sun had swelled in the west, an orange-red fireball arcing over the top of the thick green woods. It had been a long day in the sun for all. But as Father Matthew slowly walked over toward the workmen, shaking off the slumber, he finally realized that the visit of Father Steve Durković had been merely *two summers* ago. That had been at least three years *after* Father Andre's disappearance; the Skeed incident could have had nothing to do with this shipwreck. And yes, his mind had been all through this a few times before, following recurring self-accusations in his nightmares. But he still could not remember how exactly he had managed to procure *silencio* from that feckless cheerleader for the fading revolution, although he was sure he had done so. Also far as he knew, no footage of Father Durković at San Plácido had ever surfaced, nor news of that visit been disseminated.

But the realization that he had effectively protected his mission, on another occasion, from ambiguous contacts with suspicious people only, paradoxically, made Matthew's head hurt worse. It only deepened this impossible puzzle. *Why? How? Who?*

Felipe walked up to him, sweaty from daylong work. They had found even more graves. The death count was in the forties.

"Okay, we have to have all this over by tomorrow afternoon at the latest," Matthew heard his own voice coming out of himself, "The Mass will have to wait until tomorrow night, but we can do it no later. Then we must leave. Tell them that, Felipe."

"Sí, Padre."

A woman came across the plaza, handing Matthew a plate of beans and *tortillas*. He bowed gravely, thanked her. It was wonderful and finally revived him properly.

The answers to this are here, if anywhere, Matthew grimly told himself. But we may well never figure it out, or at least not now. Fine, he figured, do what you have to do. Give proper burial to these dead, and do the other things which only a priest can do. Leaving was going to be hard, of course. But we will be back soon....

Soon? He thought about that. The same military junta still ran this country, despite what they told you. Either way, you certainly had to figure on that. And while things had remained calm in conservative Cañada, you just never knew. There were still notorious killings elsewhere, mainly assassinations as far as you could tell, no more reports of mass murder. But only God knew what all had happened. You could not be careful enough. Soon? Figure carefully what you say to these people when you pull out, he cautioned himself, they are a sober people and they do not need false promises from a Roman Catholic priest.

The dream of Durković still rankled him as he came up to the open graves. Here is your work, fool, he thought, here your rhapsodic dreams of utopia as seen through the sights of a rifle, here the fruits of your "just war" as an "act of self-defense." I am going to have to have a talk with Christopher about that crazy....

Now here was a sight: six of the young men who had come down from the north, wearing t-shirts and baseball caps as if they had just landed from east L.A. All were leaning forward with shovels in a line, all down in a trench facing the same way, digging out underneath a tangle of great old tree roots. Between these roots the late sun reflected off the round pates of skulls, little groups of three or four of them like peas in pods. The mouths were fixed open in the dried mud, the irregular, off-white teeth gleaming brighter than the dull grey bone in the dying light. Now and then one would be freed, gently lifted out by a tool and slowly passed over to waiting hands. Then the boys would dig in again, the arms pushing the shovels and then the knees and elbows raising and turning, all in continuous motion like the pistons on an old railroad train.

In a smaller grave nearby, a woman in full native garb crouched over two exposed skeletons, side by side. All around the women had continued to dress themselves up for this occasion, the long vigil over their loved ones until they were properly reburied tomorrow. This woman hardly moved, did not even shake or sob, merely held her position fixedly and stared. Occasionally her hand would go out, gently dusting off the face of a skull.

Just across the way a man crouched next to a cardboard box lined with a pale sheet, carefully arranged the pieces of bone and skull inside like a jig-saw puzzle. Two Mayan women loomed over him, pointing at his work in progress and making critical gestures as they all conversed quickly and animatedly in Kekchi—no, not like that, over there. The man would move some bones and then look back up at them with his brow knitted, throwing up his hands as if to say, "What else can I do?" Dispassionately the women would either shake their heads or nod soberly—better, okay, but now fix that one....

An old woman walked briskly by carrying a heavy, gleaming silver pail full of boiled steaming chicken parts. The workers would pluck pieces out with their hands, pause briefly and refresh themselves.

A larger group was converged further to the west, Matthew saw as he walked along toward them. Here older men of this community toiled in their colored shirts and straw hats, unearthing a small group of separate pits. I wonder how any of the old men were spared, he wondered, another puzzle doubtless beyond comprehension. Beyond them lay a very large mass grave about ten yards square, five feet deep, which they had been working on all day. One old man turned toward Matthew as he approached, his brown leathery face opening up under his yellow straw hat as if to search for some answer. For it was clear that, years after this catastrophe, the village was still in shock. This is likely why they continue to hang back from me, as if uniformly spooked by my presence, Matthew told himself. For whatever else I am, I am an outsider. But he wanted to find a way to close this fracture, and end the village's reticence.

"Hand me a shovel," he directed in Kekchi.

The old man in the yellow hat bowed gravely, handed Matthew his own and stepped back out of the way. Father Matthew leapt into the pit and toiled with the men well into the night, lost in thoughts that afterwards he would never even remember.

By the time the moon rose up over the trees to the east, sounds of weeping and mourning filled the plaza. Candles and flowers had been placed by the women near all the excavations, and some stood by silently with lighted candles in hand. Free hands covering their faces, they stood there and sobbed, their bodies shaking.

It was time for sleep. Matthew and the others set aside their shovels, and the priest slowly made his way across the plaza. He waved to Felipe and Toda, as if to say, "tomorrow." He had not even much conversed with María Bon or anyone else he knew by first name all day long, he realized, anyone who might have told him more. The great, gnawing mystery remained over this desolate place. Felipe had just shaken his head, an hour ago, when Matthew had asked him yet again about Andre: nothing. And even—or especially—María Bon, while playing her old leadership role that Augustine had taught her with punctual exactitude, had herself avoided *any* further or deeper discussion with Matthew all day long. Give up, he told himself again, it's just too vast and deep. You have finally gotten played a real hand, Padre, he told himself, just carry your head up so the people can see you. Trust shattered this deeply will not return with tricks. Just let them see you. That is all you can do.

Casaroja

Near the end of the plaza was a final, broad shallow grave with a few candles planted around it. A lantern at one corner threw it all into very high relief. And in an odd way the scene was quite interesting—Mayan rugs and shawls, deeply mud stained but otherwise not much worse for the wear after five years in the ground, two torsos still rather fully dressed in brown pants and black boots, a few old beer cans doubtless tossed in by the killers, as if all here were merely refuse, stray pieces of dull white bone. And at the far right lay one last, complete corpse fully excavated but still not removed, a man laid out flat as a pancake as if a steamroller had slowly run over him, the intact skull turned to the right and the arms looped behind and underneath. Just below the groin the brown pants were still intact; over the shoulders large, colorful patches of Mayan embroidery still rested, rosy red and sea blue. The rest made a complete and fully skeletonized figure, the ribs splayed out spindily to either side like the remains of a plate of fish.

There was shouting nearby. Matthew looked up from his contemplation to see a very ancient woman mostly in shadow at the far corner, very formally dressed in full skirt and immaculate red and white *huipil*. Her emaciated face was itself practically skeletal. "Why did you go there!" she angrily declaimed at the skeleton in Kekchi, her bony finger now and then ranging into the lantern's light, shaking toward the corpse in angry condemnation, "Why did you leave me? What good did it do?"

How many times have I seen something like this, Matthew thought, since coming to this land ten years ago? "Don't let it scare you," he remembered the firm counsel of Father Augustine, the first time he had seen a Mayan woman shouting at a statue of a saint in a church, "It's their way." And so he had seen them, women and men alike, children too, arguing vocally, loudly, and with great and intense feeling with statues and paintings of the saints, even or perhaps especially with statues of Jesus and Mary. And for that matter with figures of Maximón too, the idols of the *confradías*. But never, until tonight, with the sad corpse of a loved one.

"You left us all here! What were you thinking? How could you leave us like this?"

And just for a moment, the old woman clearly noticed Matthew's presence, and recognized him as the priest. She had somehow looked up, a glint in her eye.... And what were you going to do, Matthew chastised himself, comfort her? Tell this old lady that she protested too much, must think of eternity? That she should not weep, *la violencia* was kind? Some other time, he rued...if indeed ever. For as Matthew sort of bowed to her, acknowledging her grief as best he could as he turned away, he could not mistake the fixed and quite intentional cast of that stare back at him—a glare of unmistakable hate.

Back at his little encampment he was reassured, thankfully, that some other old lady with more gentle thoughts toward him had made up his sleeping bag, left an extra blanket and ample fresh cool water, a plate of *totopostes*. Grateful for that, he prayed and let himself return to slumber. At least he knew by now that the poor grieving old lady's scorn was not deserved. He had scanned his mind and memory deep as they would permit, as critically and coldly as he was able, and found nothing whatsoever in either his overt acts or words which could have resulted in this monstrosity. Yet that voice continued to punctuate his consciousness, whether coming through the thick woods or through his just as dense dreams, he could not say—

"You left us all here! What were you thinking? How could you leave us like this?"

THE DAY OF SHADOWS

In a state of dreamless sleep Matthew for once felt himself relaxing more fully. The physical labor had helped, and his rational mind told him this even as he slept. Nevertheless a great sense of pervasive sadness filled all his soul, for while he knew he had not triggered this disaster, he also maddeningly had been unable to prevent it. You could not have prevented it even now, he devastatingly knew, for you still do not even know exactly what *it* was—why the terrible wind had been called to this place.

Of course, he did harbor suspicions. And therefore through his sleep these suspicions paraded like a series of multiple choice questions, each spoken by the mask of a different ghost. Father Augustine, his inspiration and mentor, recently under obedience to himself as prior...have you been moved ahead too swiftly, my son? That is not your fault, it is *theirs*, the distinct southern Indiana twang broke through Augustine's lips, the only part of his mask that moved. But tell me again, son, who are your masters...the abbots? San Anselmo? Archbishop Wildenmut? Suddenly Wildenmut's fox-like face loomed there before him instead, a conversation from long ago...*excellent, excellent, excellent,* young man, *excellent*.... But what exactly did you *find* in me, your Excellency? Before Matthew could cry that out, though, came the bleeding mask of Andre once more... *Alvarado...and I with him*.... Another voice? Yes, Felipe whispering... *calumnia...acusación falsa*.... Yes, of course, all false, all lies? But from where?

The answers did not follow, and Father Matthew found himself praying in his sleep, through all this oppressive sadness. Dear Jesus, restore Your order. Show Your face, Your justice! Give me the strength—the discernment. It is all dark—I see nothing! *What went wrong?* I must see to lead, to carry out Your work here. Bless me with insight, with the facts I need. Lift up Your unworthy servant, my Lord and King! Hold nothing back!

And out of the grey fog of Matthew's fathomless restlessness suddenly shone a light—a ray from that lantern? Look closer— bright gold, not the color of fire but of something unearthly. It was descending, descending toward him and growing in size and clarity. What a wonder! Even before he could make out its shape or identify it, it was deeply calming, beautiful, imbued with God's absolute majesty and glory. It radiated a warmth, out of this world, above all things, above even this tragedy. Matthew felt his whole self become lighter, as if rising, floating up to touch it. It descended still, turning slowly toward him. A jewel case? An ancient casket of riches? No! He saw it clear and true at last: the grand old main altar at Saint Benedict's Abbey. Like a long rectangular palace, with the roof coming to five gables, the longest at center holding a gold crucifix above the tabernacle. It turned more slowly at last to fully face him as he ascended to the plane in space where it came to rest, and once again, after two decades, he saw the two levels of niches depicting saints of the Eucharist either side of center, eight saints on each side rendered in enamel. Brilliant stones and jewels glowed from all lines of the enormous gold structure, embedded in it, all in all a perfect replica of the ancient Treasury Chamber in Cologne Cathedral, the height of the sacred art of the Middle Ages.

As the altar radiantly glowed before him and Matthew found himself walking up to it, he saw it joined and supported by a long table of grey-blue marble, six Roman columns along its façade with an embossed medallion of the Triumphant Lamb at center, the Alpha to the left and the Omega to the right. *And I approach to the left*...Matthew realized, as if moving and thinking in rapt slow motion in his ecstatic wonder, *and I am not alone.* For three were walking toward the altar of God, Father Augustine the celebrant at center, himself and Christopher to either side, boys again, dressed in surplices as altar servers....

They were kneeling, before the resplendent gold altar glowing out into the surrounding dark....

"Introibo ad altare Dei," came the strong Latin of Father Augustine as they in perfect unison completed the sign of the cross. "I will go in to the altar of God."

"Ad Deum qui laetificat juventútem meam." Christopher and Matthew answered together, "The God of my gladness and joy."

"Judica me, Deus, et discérne causam meam de gente non sancta...."

Yes, Matthew found himself moving his lips in his sleep, "Judge me, O God, and distinguish my cause from the nation that is not holy: deliver me from the unjust and deceitful man...."

"Qui tu es Deus, fortitúdo me," he was speaking out loud, intoning the 42nd Psalm with Christopher, *"Why Oh God hast Thou cast me off? And why do I go sorrowful whilst the enemy afflicteth me?"*

Still lost more in wonder than mourning, Matthew remained transfixed before the clarity of this memory, clear and brilliant as the precious stones gleaming from the altar—ruby red, turquoise, sea green—

But as he heard Father Augustine solemnly reciting the Confiteor, a sense of mourning returned, only deepened—

"...quia peccávi nimus cogitatióne verbo, et opere: that I have sinned exceedingly in thought, word, and deed...."

And Matthew found tears welling his eyes as it was his and Christopher's turn to take up the same prayer, repeat it word for word as, bowing low together, they turned left and right, striking their breasts three times—

"Mea culpa, mea culpa, mea máxima culpa," he heard his young boy's voice rising up now, and it was as if scales had fallen from his eyes. Had this been the moment, his rational mind rifled through this memory deep in sleep, when *my own thick skull had finally been penetrated—but not by Death but by Light? By the knowledge that this was a moment in eternity timeless and enduring, that we actually then and there were present at Calvary? And at all Masses ever said in all times past, or to be said in all times future? That indeed time was abolished amidst this sacred cadence, that in the ever-renewed sacrifice of the Body and Blood of Christ we were entering an eternal, unchangeable, unalterable moment? And present forever as this memory still is to me?*

"Through my fault, through my fault, through my most grievous fault!" Matthew felt himself shouting out loud, competing consciously with the angry declamations of that old woman by the grave tonight, "Take them all up with You, Lord, into Your timelessness! To this Your altar they are Yours! Your people—we baptized them—tended them—Augustine, myself, Andre—take them up! Gather them to Yourself! Wash their blood away in Your own! Bring them home!"

* * *

Awake at his campsite, Father Matthew for once felt physically rested. The last images of his dreams still lingered before him; he shook them off. He heard the sound of shovels and shouts in the distance. *Tortillas* and coffee were set out nearby for him. *Gracias*, he thought, to my helpful angel, whoever you are.

Shortly he emerged from the woods out onto the plaza. The sky was uniformly grey, the whole world today shadowed. But it was somewhat cooler. He was determined to get this business of reburial concluded, and then to get grimly on. The figure of Felipe appeared out before him.

Matthew stopped; he started to speak but need not have. Felipe by now could well read his face. "Andre—?"

"Nada, Padre." Felipe stated it sadly.

So this is the way it is going to be, Matthew figured. He decided to be resigned to it, much as his nature resisted that mode. No, you're going to have to leave here without answers, he practiced telling himself. Or just settle for simple ones: the general national violence back in the early 1980s, the leftist guerillas at large in the mountains, the lunatic and edgy military, "red house." It was all stupid, of course, but what legitimate reason or explanation could ever exist for mass murder anyway? In the deepest sense, it did not matter "why." He was a priest; his anointed hands had more essential tasks to perform, and in a whole other dimension. The glorious memory of that altar at old Saint Benedict's buoyed up his spirit, carried him along now.

The priest simply found a shovel, and took up again as he had the day before. The still very reticent people made room for him. It seemed that virtually all the graves had been located. What remained was to identify some victims, make them whole as possible, reverently lay them out with the small pieces of boxes and board in the great grave Matthew had directed.

Women were everywhere this grey day, all in their colorful best again, mourning. In the new grave that Father Matthew would bless later this evening, many of the dead were already laid out carefully with bunches and baskets of flowers between them, and at their heads and feet. The bodies were dressed as best they could, sometimes with fresh bandanas and scarves wrapped around their skulls. Small candles were stuck in the dirt all around them, lit and glowing against the day's dull cast. The people had also become more efficient in fighting off the scavenging birds, groups of boys going after them with rugs and sticks.

The villagers, however cool to the priest personally, nevertheless had more babies for him to baptize, more couples to marry in the middle of the day. More people had come down from the north, some just to watch and join in the general mourning, and to pray with the women around the dead and give comfort. Matthew duly donned his surplice and stole once again and performed all the sacraments as reverently as he knew how. These new ones are charismatics, he could clearly discern, always eager to smile and sing but their catechesis thin to the point of non-existence. Have to deal with that later, he knew, whenever that might be. Felipe carefully wrote down the names and ages of all the newly found dead, all the newly baptized babies and married couples and all witnesses in Matthew's ledger book, as he had been instructed.

Matthew once more found himself making vague statements about being back here soon, continuing to work with them. But he found his voice cracking a little today, as if it was a remnant of his voice from adolescence. He had become somewhat detached, under the enormity of the tragedy here and the vastness of the work to do and redo. He did not feel the same blush of confidence as yesterday; he recognized that and shrewdly did his best to keep his troubled spirit well hid. Hard to say what all that was—his own suspicion of this charismaticism, however enthusiastic it was on the surface, a more realistic and penetrating analysis of the difficulties at hand, now that he had been here a couple of days, or a reaction to the ever more obvious and almost physical distance that many, far too many of the survivors of this village yet maintained from him, the strange downcast glow in their eyes when you looked toward them and their tendency to then instantly look away. Maybe less hard to say than not wanting to say, he knew....

The priest could only more hesitate to acknowledge to himself, however, how something of his own aura only found reflection and like response in this wary reaction of the people. He did sense it dimly and knew exactly what it was: the gaping absence of Father Andre Meinrad Mondragon, O.S.B. Where are you, my monk, Matthew almost found himself shouting at one point. The person of Andre had resonated through his consciousness all through that long journey, and to the extent it was an irritant it had spurred him on. And then this. Total absence—amidst devastation, amidst permanently scarred memories and faith rocked to the roots, amidst dozens of innocent dead. *You* should be doing these blessings, Pastor Andre, Matthew wanted to accuse his charge, *you* should be the one hearing the loud complaints of these women declaiming their dead. Whatever bonko theology you were drinking, whatever floridly verbose, ultra-utopian impossibilities and Teilhardian anthro-speak, none of it provides an iota of an excuse!

As for what he was going to report to Archabbot Kreidler or Archbishop Wildenmut, Prior Matthew Eberhard cared not at all. The thought only more deeply scoured the bedrock of his anger, his rising gorge and absolute disgust. You brothers in Saint Benedict, where did *your* priest go? Where is he now, your high school science project gone haywire? For as Matthew's dawning sense of the horror's dimensions and roots came more fully clear, and the secondary nature of his own personal negligence, the pre-eminent and blatantly active fault of his superiors only shone more the brightly.

It was enough to make you cry.... But blessedly, the old altar of Saint Benedict's came descending once more from darkness, swept up all his frustration and deflected emotion. In Christ, yes! All in Christ, throw all confusion at His cross! Only You, Lord can set this whole and complete. Look here, how these magnificent people shadow the work of Your own Divine Hand, attempt to lovingly

Casaroja

rejoin the broken bones of their loved ones! All only in You, all only through You!

At two o'clock Father Matthew ceased his labors, seeing that all was finally complete. He used up two of Salazar's disposable cameras. Then, as on the day before, he found the old red chair, had a shot of Basil Hayden's, savored its well-aged sweetness. Again he carefully leaned back, just a bit, against that remnant of the wall of San Tomás. And as sleep came quickly, thankfully for once he did not dream.

* * *

Matthew looked at his watch: three-forty. He would have to begin preparing for the Mass before long. He noticed the big cross he had directed yesterday had been finished and laid nearby. He saw Felipe taking notes about thirty yards away.

"Felipe!"

He came over. "Sixty-one," Felipe reported. "They are almost done. Perhaps another hour or so."

"Yes," Matthew said, "tell them the Mass will have to start later, about seven. Also tell them to dig a deep hole for the cross in the middle of the floor of the old church."

"Sí, Padre Matthew."

The priest stood up, feeling as if the whole world was moving in slow motion. It was as if all energy had flowed out of him, as if something enormous and invisible had passed right through him. He was not only no longer tired, though, but for once felt positively energized, his old self. How strange. And he was just as strangely very clear-headed. It was only that suddenly, all sound and all images seemed very very slow, as if suspended in a thick translucent atmosphere.

The new mass grave was a staggering sight. The skeletons were set in rows of five, the heads facing east as he had instructed. All skulls had been re-set with bodies, all laid out straight and supine. Every single one of them was now clothed with headbands, flowers, candles, decorations of many sorts. There were no coffins as such, but many were placed on the top of blankets, or had the cardboard or wood built around them. They would lay many blankets atop all of them, when the graves were closed; as proper a burial as you could manage was very important to Mayans.

The mourning continued, some loud, much silent and tender. There was that and then there was the astonishing, almost surreal counterpoint of the orderliness of the five long rows of bodies, which looked positively festive. This is exactly as Matthew had wanted it; he had decreed it in those other, smaller crime scenes he had been to these several years. But never before had there been more than a dozen. Dear, dear Lord: here is the whole harvest of souls we have tended for over two decades in this place, here is a large part of our lives' work. It would only be visible for a few more hours, the day about to end, but they would never forget it now: all of the victims together, a city of the dead, the final, horrific aloneness of each loved one erased, the disorder and contempt banished by the best loving hands could once more do, one last time.

All the men were working. There were a few dozen of them digging out the last ones. They were actually going to finish the job. Matthew picked up a shovel once more, helped with a few: bodies curled into the dense, fine soil, holding themselves in fetal positions. Dirt filling up mouths, caked inside rows of stained brownish teeth. Remembering Salazar again, Matthew pulled out his last disposable camera and clinically shot off all but a few remaining frames. What is this, he wondered, this final evidence, hellishly discarded like refuse by minds impossible to imagine? The final postures retained, the chests and torsos sometimes still encased with clothes that outlasted their wearers? Only a massive, numbing silence, the overall tragedy plain but the individual stories beyond reach. Blessedly too, of course. But the entire picture suggested nothing so much as the ruins of a great fire, raging and hungry, insatiable as long as it had lasted.

Death, death: Matthew had encountered it enough times and in a maddening variety of ways in his years as a priest. Most often simple homely sorrows, sometimes sudden but usually stretched out and ritualized into the onset of illness, the long letting go, the final days. He had seen murder, too, in more than one context by now. You never forgot one of them, long as you lived, or any of the details no matter how brief your encounter. Nor Satan's mockery, his challenge: *see,*

Casaroja

this is all there is, look at him. You set up something over me, priest? You speak to a higher claim? What except slaughter and decay, utter extinction? Occasionally you quietly replied. But more often, Matthew grimly knew, you just nimbly side-stepped it all, passed the demon like a matador. The absolute hollowness, the element of surprise often left you little other course. But it always exposed something in you, too, when you handled it that way. Especially when you side-stepped it not out of surprise or necessity, but consciously. And especially as a priest.

The Prince of Murders could burn you, Matthew had learned very early, and it was a good lesson too. You survived it and thereafter were watchful not to let him have at you that way again, if you could help it. He still recalled his first encounter with it very well, looking at those brown bones. It had been just after his ordination, back at Saint Benedict's one beautiful day in June in Southern Indiana, full and lush. Boys had encountered a half-buried skull in a cornfield; the sheriff went out and exhumed a young man who had disappeared two summers earlier from the town. It had always been assumed he had run away, but it quickly developed he had been murdered by two friends. All three were in their early twenties, all three Catholic. And all three had been using various drugs, it turned out.

Matthew had been called in because the parish priest was on vacation. He vaguely recalled the victim's family and that of one of the killers; they had occasionally been up at the abbey for Sunday Mass. The victim's body had been buried on the wooded outskirts on his own parents' farm, for whatever reason, adding to their shock and horror: he had been out there all that time. Also, like these dead today, some of his clothes had oddly outlasted his flesh: he was found wearing a ridiculous rock concert T-shirt with ugly cartoons of dragons. His family went into a stupor; the mother prayed hard but the father let something go, very deep, some key aspect of his faith shattered. The killers' families had more profound reactions, deeply penitent, numb too but on another level now fully awake. The boys had not been above reproach but they had no arrest records either, of any sort. But these killers' parents ultimately saw it all, and horrible as it was, they came to terms.

The first killer, who had actually done the deed, turned to stone.

The boy had probably been that way already but now the mask fell off. He said nothing, sat immobile staring at the walls of his cell. He was far beyond reach.

The other, who had goaded him on, handed him the weapon—a ball bat—and created the opportunity, was the key. He was the favorite of all the parents, a decent student and industrious worker, already at 22 a popular local personality. He retained all of this after his arrest. The motive? No one knew. They had not been in fear of arrest for drugs at all, their sellers were several miles north. The detective spoke of a "frenzy" the night of the killing, the usual drugs plus loud music. But that was close as they got.

"Good afternoon, Father," this one said, in all apparent sincerity, as he was brought into a jail visiting room where the young Father Matthew had waited.

"Good afternoon."

"Huh, well…" The boy sat there awhile, occasionally scratching his head, as if embarrassed at being speechless. Matthew assured him there was no hurry; he was here to offer what spiritual aid as he could.

"Spiritual aid…is that anything like Kool-Aid, Father?"

Matthew did not reply. Just brushed it off, tried to appear unruffled and patient. Doubtless, the fellow was very mixed up, nervous, conflicted, God knew what.

"Ah…" He started singing advertising jingles from television, for children's breakfast cereal. "Maybe not too good, huh? What about this?" Then here came the Oscar Meyer weiner song… then he stopped abruptly. And then he started singing another one, putting himself into a melodic falsetto. Then went right into another. Matthew watched, expressionless. "Oh, it's no use," the young killer entreated the rookie priest, "I know them all, you know, they never stop. They're all rattlin' around up here, you know…" his voice dropped, suddenly, monstrously, *"in my skull."* He was sitting there pointing to his head.

Matthew had never seen it before. But *it* knew, faster than a spark of electricity. Eyes brightened, without blinking or moving at all.

"Don't dwell on that…" Matthew's voice had trailed off. And he

Casaroja

had realized before all his words came out that he had already lost. He was being reactive, dodging. He was not here to be a therapist. As it knew. And it was lightning.

"Not a problem," the boy's utterly cool, suave, friendly social exterior returned, "Gee, I guess I really don't appreciate a lot of things enough, you know, how you all are really tryin' to help me." He smiled.

And that was the end of the interview. For that day, and for all time. Matthew had missed the real encounter. He had not possessed the readiness for it. The boy had then been convicted and sent away to state prison for life. After about a year, Matthew heard that he had hung himself. When back at Saint Benedict's for a visit once, Matthew made it a point to go out and visit the parents. Toughened, even hardened yet with a compassion beyond imagining, they showed Matthew the suicide note: "I need a challenge." They had hoped, by showing it to him, to give some reassurance: that the boy had been beyond human contact, that there was nothing Matthew could have done. Matthew thanked them, kissed them, blessed them. Then went back to the abbey and prayed far into the night: Lord, Lord, drive out whatever remnant of this beast which clings to me! For it certainly did; Matthew could feel the sting. "I need a challenge." Indeed, Matthew rued, someone other than *myself*. And forgive me Lord, this creature was a work of beauty to Your eye when You made him, and in some unfathomable way You held out Your love and mercy to him until the day he refused You forever. And I let this treasure slip through my hands, I your priest, excuse my abject negligence....

And now this...the count was up to 63....

All right, enough, he told himself. I need one more small spot of sleep, there is so much still ahead—the Mass for the dead, the burials, then packing and getting on the horse, not sleeping until tomorrow morning and going back as far on that road again as I can, and as fast....

Matthew put down his shovel and walked slowly back to the broken wall. *Another shot of Hayden's, Padre?* Forget it, later. But it was marvelous, a great gift from God, the way the sands seemed to shift in your head when you tilted the chair back and leaned there, just so....

*   *   *

"Padre Matthew...."

He was startled awake...what had passed over the sun? What time was it? Almost five....

"Padre Matthew...there is something you have to see."

Matthew awoke to the face of Felipe. He was utterly serious, somber. There could be no question but to follow him. Just behind Felipe was an old man that Matthew was slow to recognize, but who he then recalled as the man María Bon had been demonstratively arguing with earlier. A very old man in brown shirt and hat. And behind him, in the distance, waited another, an ancient man. The very postures of these old men were a quick study: survivors, God knew how.

"Fine," Matthew said, "Let's go." He picked up his pack.

They motioned to the ancient fellow, almost a copy of the old man in brown but perhaps twenty years older. He turned and headed off toward an opening in the forest, south of the plaza. All followed closely.

They had not very far to go at all, perhaps a mile and a half at most. The forest path was narrow and close, meandering slowly uphill. They fell into single file, no one saying anything. The path began to rise more, turn to the right. A hill emerged, low domed, ahead. The trees fell away and the path climbed it diagonally, decidedly to the right.

They followed the two old men across the hill's flat, open crest, just to the opening of another woods on the other side. There they stopped, before a small Mayan altar. While you could not say it had been used recently, it was not abandoned, either. There were some old remnants of charcoal around the edges of the stone hearth, potsherds, and some small bones. The old business, Matthew mused, lightning in the blood and all the rest. All waited patiently while the priest inspected this place, but it seemed merely of tangential interest to them. No way to say what exactly had been going on here, Matthew saw, doubtless no more than the usual. It did not appear to involve a very big group, likely just the shaman and a few followers at most. What am I going to do, knock it down? Priests had been doing that here for over three hundred years. It would not do any good; they always came back. But he took some exorcised water out of his pack, meditatively spread it all over and said the Saint Michael's prayer.

They all moved on. They came to a point perhaps a hundred yards downslope where the forest was still open, a patch of greying sky above. As they approached it began to look like something of a debris field, old bottles and parts of bottles littered about, half-emerged from the soil. Two men were at work here with shovels, exposing a curled trench in the shape of a backward letter S. The grave diggers stopped their work, quietly stepped aside. Four skeletons had been exposed out of the mud and odd litter here, all male.

Matthew stepped up to the rim of the trench. A slender skeleton was face down, its right arm slightly reaching out over the head, as if blessing the other three thrown randomly below it in all odd poses. A knot of hemp still clung to the right wrist bone; the back of the face-down skull was open. Matthew did believe he recognized the remnant of the bluejean shirt. Yes, and the black pants were standard issue.

"Turn him over," Father Matthew directed.

They did so. The black leather shoes were more apparent, also standard issue. And you could see a small hole in the center of the forehead, obviously the entrance wound. An execution.

Everyone stood far back from Matthew as he stepped into the grave and crouched low. Little ants and centipedes, very, very small, were still doing their work, moving very slowly around the granules of dirt and clay, sticking close to the base. Funny that they still found occupation, after all this time. The smell was of pungent, stinging tar, the old familiar smell of the human dead that no animal ever carried. Its eyes were gone, the brown skull very clean, the mouth stoically closed and the white, well-maintained teeth fixed. A remembered pair of round eyeglasses, broken, lay nearby.

Turning over the body had exposed two round objects the size of half-dollars. They lay to the right of the chest in the dirt. Matthew dug out the first with his nails, finding it still attached to a piece of black string that wound back to the man's shoulder. A medallion of some sort. He stood up, spit on it, took out his hanky and scraped out its shape. A carved profile of a man's face, stalwart, made by ridged outline, almost cartoon-like. Two words, one to either side of the outlined head:

```
   BEN     A
   ED      B
   IC      BO
    T      T
```

It was that late 60s version of the Saint Benedict medal that had been all the rage. He flipped it over and found the familiar outline of the thick cross, a plus sign proclaiming from its center:

```
     P E A C E
```

That was all; the bold modern design left no room for the exorcism prayer.

The second medal was of the same style and material, another cartoonish portrait framed by a name:

```
    M       H
   EIN     ER
   RA     MI
    D       T
```

And on the back side, two black ravens.

Matthew stooped closer to the corpse, fingered through the dirt around the skull. No bullets, no other clues. The party continued to watch him silently as he carefully did his work. He noticed Felipe very close above the pit, his face having settled into a mask of perfect, sublime mournfulness. But this is beyond even great sorrow, Matthew mused, this is far beyond any familiar emotion, anywhere I have even really been before, true *terra incognita*. *Something is here though*, he felt, somehow. It was an almost insane thought, from absolute nowhere. The second raven speaking to me, he thought, yesterday afternoon—that bold one. He let this flash of madness extend farther. *The one I had not seen until the first one leapt off the chair.* Pray for me, Saint Meinrad, he found himself jumping back to his prayer from yesterday afternoon, let these ravens teach me more about your namesake, as your own loyal ravens taught the people of your murder.

Perhaps the skull itself....

Matthew picked it up, looked long into its gaze. Just above the grave's rim he also saw, again, Felipe's face, that healthy brown Hispanic flesh, deeply lined by his emotion, adding a strange, somewhat distracting counterpoint. "Ah, poor Andre!" Matthew heard himself saying right out loud, as detached from his own body as this skull was from its. "Yes, Felipe, this is him. Much like you, I'd say too. A fellow of no sense of humor whatsoever." Felipe finally grinned, albeit a tough little flash, too brief. "What I need you to do is think, Felipe. You have talked to many more people here than I and time is short. Why are these bodies here separate from all others? Does it have something to do with that altar, for instance? Or is it something else?"

"No one spoke of the old religion here," Felipe said, "not to Toda, either, Padre Matthew. I think it is only *coincidencia*. But this is a place apart...and from what I can see of our Faith that is still in the village, if anyone knew of the old ways, that altar would have been as especially apart as we found it."

Matthew agreed. But what he was really doing, without letting Felipe know it, was watching the impact of his actions on the faces of those two strange old Kekchi men, who obviously had known something of this site. He had remembered them when he had remembered the ravens, and the degree of that passionate vehemence in the first man's discussion yesterday with María Bon. Seeming to maintain his gaze upon the skull, the priest continued carefully scanning those two old faces during this exchange with

Felipe, looking for so much as a flinch. But unlike Felipe's, the faces of these *indígena* remained total masks, as absolutely expressionless as this skull. *Play it a little farther, Padre,* something told him, though. *You have been in this country long enough yourself, now, to know that such masks are a statement in themselves.* Yes, Matthew realized, they know....

He fingered the hole in the forehead with his little finger...*just that small*.... Where are your evolving paradigms of eschatological experience now, Father Mondragon? Your praxis of communitarian struggle and engaged love? He turned the skull in his hands, completely over. The shattering exit wound behind made it bowl-like, a brown walnut colored dish half-full of black grained dirt. "Are you liberated now?" Matthew allowed himself to sing a little, "*El acto de librar,*" he enunciated carefully, penetrating the dead, hot, thick afternoon air. Yes, as they said, Spanish is the loving tongue. And they were right. For while this thing in his hands was tongueless and fleshless, Matthew had just then seen, out the corner of his eye, two pairs of old fleshy, Kekchi ears react perfectly, in their bat-like way, to his performance.

He shook the brown bowl; nothing metal popped out, no bullet or fragments. As evidence, it was still pretty thin gruel. Or thin brains...is *this* where all that daring theology ended, all those breathtaking constructions of pseudo-mystical verbiage? Ah, be careful Matthew, he said to himself, this poor soul also actually read your own book, that too has passed through several worms' stomachs into this. Ugghh, dear sweet Jesu! What a purgatory! Yet doubtless *this* is what accounts for the precise grade and flavor of the death smell here, accounts for its particular ability to sting our own still-living eyes. And remember too, pilgrim, yours are not yet, by any yardstick, tears of penitence. Yugghh! Though certainly, too, this is what must account for that deepest smell, yes, which is so like something you do not right now even want to mention to yourself....

Well, there will have to be hair shirts aplenty later, or something along those lines. Thinking of his own rotten graduate thesis, Matthew just disgustingly splashed out the skull's contents on the ground—still no bullet. Nothing but dirt raining on dirt, words, words,

Casaroja

words.... And the two Kekchi men seemed singularly unimpressed by his performance, perhaps were on to the game.

Matthew quickly went through Father Andre's shirt pocket. Nothing. Then all the rest of his pockets. Nothing. And nothing more from the stone-faced Kekchi, either.

All right, all right, go back to square one, he figured. Take it real slow. You know something is here. *They* know something is here. And there they stand, the two of them. Plus the two grave diggers, plus Felipe, who is still thinking real hard. Making five of them in total, but be careful with that numbers business. Remember what happened when they got into that sort of thing way back when, on our old beloved "Hill," in the bad old days. But just for the sake of the elementary, Sherlock, five. And four of them here in this hole, Andre plus three. But, come to think of it, actually five at this moment. Five, that is, including me: me standing in this grave. Me and the dead here, then, have no numerical physical advantage, and these poor rotten fellows were obviously quite outnumbered when this all happened. But at least right at this moment we are evenly matched in the invisible realm of the spirit, against these my spooked, silent companions. Come on, dusty fellows, he tried to pray, talk to me, I am on your side for the moment. If only I could unlock what you ghosts have to tell me....

He looked up at the five stony living faces. He continued to relish the silence. He was searching them carefully, letting them know it. And they are waiting, he saw....

Yes. That was it. Five of them there, five of us here. Something less on this side, for sure: four dead. But something more, too. For I am a priest, and they acknowledge it. I am Father Matthew Eberhard, and they brought me here. Willingly too, though they say little. They gave themselves away, however, back on that hilltop. For if they are not impressed by my bumbling, my activity in this pit, they were even less impressed by that Aztec stone. No, they are not partakers of the lightning in the blood. They are partakers of the Body of Christ; yes, of course. Just very silent. Very canny. They are afraid, after all. With certainly plenty to be afraid of.

And as he continued to try to boil it down to the most elemental, something vital came over Matthew suddenly, with a warm tide of recognition, a true-living spark here among the dead. And it was simply this: just how much of that fear he himself had picked up, registered, in the short time here. From the five living men up along the rim. An understandable fear, of course. *But something else in it, too*. What was it? These two very canny old men, very practiced survivors, were not saying. Just look at those faces, dear Jesus, what masterpieces of Your craft! And I, your feckless priest cannot even read them, these virtual spooks.

But I wonder, are they *honest* spooks? They have to be. But just how?

Two plus two plus one. The two old ones impenetrable. Down here, one plus four. The four silent. But really, *he* was a priest too, poor Andre. Still is, wherever he is, God help him. So look at it as one plus one plus three.... Yes. Yes....

And then, as if from nowhere, a recollected vision hit him square. The *other* raven, in a place apart. The *other* three in this trench....

Matthew let himself sway a little, scan the rest of the grave site. And I have not even looked at them yet.... Though certainly, the trail with poor Father Andre had grown cold. Matthew moved gingerly down the circling trench toward the other dead. The party above and across the trench did not speak, but followed.

Two of these other three deads were obviously native here, by skull, body shape and clothing. They were just like all the others out on the plaza, to all appearances. There was nothing in their pockets either, or around them. No clues. But the third? The bones had been stained to the same color by the earth, but the whole frame seemed bigger than his two companions in death. Certainly hardly even a medium sized American, but perhaps an Hispanic? It was hard to say. The skull just looked at you differently, that was all. It was not even anything you could put into words. The clothing was somehow a different texture, what was left of it. Hard to say.... And nothing in the pockets, either....

Time was running out, for sure. They had to get out of here very soon if he was going to get the Mass in tonight. And there was going to be no question about that. It is too late, we have to get moving. He reluctantly forced himself out of the grave.

But it's here: it's here. What is this, Matthew thought, am I

Casaroja

going mad? No: go back to the drill. You are the priest. And all the others are watching very intently now, very intently indeed. The two old men especially. Slow, slow. For I am working from a very old, timeworn script. One ancient as all the world, for sure. Trying to put flesh I cannot even imagine upon bones I do not even have time properly to know. Brown bones, red-black dirt. White teeth. Blue shirts, two of them. Perhaps once blue, this third, hard to say. And white—there? What is that?

Matthew jumped back into the grave. No, the third man had not been released completely from the ground yet. *That was where they had been working when we came in.*

"Give me a shovel!"

One was handed to him, instantly. And in that gesture, Father Matthew Eberhard, O.S.B., looked directly at the two old Kekchi. Their eyes like piercing fire, noses flaring. Silence even stonier, but silence that was starting finally to speak. Of what? Hate? No, though you could mistake it for that. Anger? Well, perhaps in part.... *Why??*

He dug at the white part; shoes finally appeared, pointed out in either direction. Not like any of the others, anywhere today. Very dirty, stained through and through. Matthew leaned down and spit harshly at them, at the soles, again and again. Just wiped it off on his pants. Perhaps this anger was catching. Wiped, spit again: *there*. Yes, white soles.

He pulled one off with some effort, held it up close to his face. Spit yet more, repeatedly, digging with his nails and rubbing with the side of his hand. There it was; it said something. Finally spat and wiped it all clean, read it:

ADIDAS

Okay, sure, you are not dreaming. For you have seen color in your dreams many times, pilgrim, despite what all the studies say. And seen many wonderful things in those dreams, too, and also terrible things. But never once, in any dream, smelled. And I am smelling now, for sure. Yes, this is definitely deep in the jungles of Alta Verapaz, Guatemala, an actual place. And this is a larger than ordinary skeleton with a different color shirt and white running shoes. Buried slightly apart from a priest, next to two others; these other three apart. In a place apart. Where I was brought by two men who are believing Catholics, but do not speak. Obey, and answer, but only when asked.

Father Matthew looked at those two faces, and saw....

And his heart, suddenly red-hot, flamed and seemed to fall through him, fall through the grave, it was so heavy, as if to go deeply down into the earth with these dead. *Dear gentle Jesus, I am sorry, I am sorry but I know not why....*

For when he had seen those two Kekchi again he had seen fire, their faces and profiles perfect flames. Their eyes the blue of a flame's core. And the silence that spoke was the silence not of hate, nor of anger, but of fear beyond anything he had ever dreamed— *fear of me, the priest!* Not as an outsider, not even as a negligent superior, but *as a priest*. And so, the priest finally knew. *That is what I have been seeing all along*. For these two men reminded Matthew of nothing so much as Toda, that night on the ridge when Matthew had first revealed himself to the *indígena*. The two old ones here looked exactly as he. But why that fear? Why, why?

No time for such brainstorming.

"Who are these three men?" Matthew heard his own voice ring out. He had not even thought through the words. He was recalling the suspicious Toda's suddenly fierce loyalty, when he had for once heard the voice of command.

"Friends of Marcos," the oldest man stated plainly.

What?? Marcos? Who in....

"Who is Marcos?" Matthew's voice rang into the woods again, "¿Quién es *Marcos?*"

The two old men looked as if they were suddenly struck dumb, pillars of salt. Only the eyes remained molten, widening, boiling. That may well have been hate, straight out of nowhere. Some impossible hate was at the bottom of this. *Well I hate it too*, Matthew began to rage deep inside, thinking of the 63 back on the plaza, the four here including his own priest, his own and Christ's soldier, wayward or no. *I hate it too*, he thought, as if to begin roiling into his own pillar of salt, *and take a look at me, too!*

Casaroja

No, it is a long time since that pathetic, evil farm boy in his jail cell, long ago—

"*I asked you who is Marcos!!*" Matthew let his rage peal, curling and growling like a deadly cat in this jungle, a tone not even lost when his voice reverberated back from the circle of trees.

They wavered and shook, all five of them, as against the outburst of a great wind. But now, restored to its former tone if not the same strength or timbre, the little ancient man's voice came across, with a sense of disbelief innocently trailing under the awed obedience....

"Padre Andre's friend…we…we…."

It was unintelligible to Matthew.

"Yes?" the priest said, understandingly but still clearly imperative.

"They are very sorry, very sorry, Padre Matthew," Felipe translated, "They beg your forgiveness. They thought you knew."

"Sure, of course," Matthew said. And tried to keep from swaying, himself, in this awesome aftershock. Or at least from looking like he was swaying, as he felt his ignited heart glow and enlarge, again. This big, Jesus, this big? As big as all my world here, as this whole mission we carry on in Your name? For it was no ordinary fear, of course, and not even fear on the scale of a massacre. For it has that other dimension: *I am a priest*. In a sense, their priest. *Who they all have come to fear, for their very lives*. I will never get to the bottom of it today, for sure…friends of Marcos, Father Andre's friend…. What was any of this?

Swooning, Matthew just went through motions. But oh, thank you Jesus, for giving me these motions....

Matthew leapt out and around to the other side of the grave, and stood before the two Kekchi. He took out holy water and blessed them, blessed them all. They all made the sign of the cross. Matthew bade them all kneel down together, and led them through some prayers. For there was no other way to deal with this monster that had been revealed in their presence. That had seized center stage in this community, destroyed the very deepest trust in all dimensions.

Then quickly, time to pay the piper. Matthew went back in and searched the third man's pockets again: nothing. No more clues. Then took out his last disposable camera, shot pictures of Father

Andre Meinrad Mondragon in his grave. There, Salazar should like that. He walked over to the other three....

No....

That sense from out of the blue, again. *Definitely not.* He used up the last two shots on Andre, careful not to show any of the surrounding area or landscape. And that is what you are entitled to, Professor. I have rendered unto Caesar, for today. The rest is not yours. I do not know who, in that dimension beyond your own, to render it to. But we will do that rendering later.

Matthew walked over to the third stranger's body, picked up that awful Adidas shoe. He instinctively stuck it in his backpack, noticing that it contained a more or less complete foot.... *Aghh.* But enough to give you a complete—and secret—Catholic burial, Jacko, when I get back to San Placido, Matthew thought. And yeah, kid, he told himself, your instincts run ahead of even your reason, Augustine always said so. So *where* are they leading you?

He walked back to the group.

"What are the names of the three?"

"Banto and Geraldo are the two natives."

"What about the other?"

There was silence.

"They know not the third friend of Marcos," Felipe said.

"You mean the third one *isn't* Marcos?"

"No. Marcos was not here when any of this happened."

"Was this third fellow here *ladino* or Spanish?"

"Neither."

"What was Marcos?"

"*Americáno.*"

"*Americáno?* Are they sure?"

"There is no doubt of it, Padre Matthew."

"Describe him."

That pause again.

Okay, Matthew thought. No rage this time. But do what they appreciate. That imperativeness.

"Describe Marcos, *por favor*." He said it slowly and with deep gravity. And saw the oldest man nod. Wonderful, they were honest spooks.

Casaroja

"Un padre."

"No...." Now you doubly knew the root of this distrust, Matthew thought ruefully. "Andre's friend." Who I never even heard of.

"Definitely, Padre Matthew, a priest," Felipe continued to translate carefully, "And certainly an *americáno*. Big man, barrel chested. Blue eyes and sandy colored hair. Friendly at first...not always afterwards."

"Where was he from?"

The old men both visibly shrugged.

"They have no idea. They thought he was from where you are from."

"When was he seen last?"

"Before the massacre. Not long before. These were his disciples...."

"I see."

"The third disciple?"

"Not of this country. *Americáno* maybe...but not Anglo. They know not what."

"Where were the disciples from?"

"Banto and Geraldo from here. The third disciple of Marcos they know not from where. He appeared one day with Marcos. They had never seen him before that."

"They say disciples of Marcos and not of Padre Andre?"

"Sí. So they say exactly."

"And of what did this discipleship consist?"

"They know not what. It was secret. And they had no interest in Marcos' talk."

"His *talk*?"

"They went to the first one and never went back," Felipe patiently explained. "These old men are father and son, you see. They agree on everything; people call them twins, the twin saints, *santos*," Felipe emphasized, also emphasizing that the villagers here had borrowed that term from the Spanish for the two old men, "for their *discretion*, Padre. The *santos* had no use for Marcos, it is obvious to me, Padre Matthew. They are deeply gratified to hear you never knew him. You have grown very esteemed in their eyes since they have learned this."

"I thank them. Ask them why Padre Marcos was not esteemed."

And suddenly, an incredible sight. The second old *santo*, the son, started walking around the grave. An exaggerated, rolling gait, like Chaplin. With his arms cracked at the elbows to suggest the man's bulk. And a face beyond the pale: an impossible meld of phony cheer, gross stupidity, sneering superiority. Strutting around with that look, even using the grave as part of the act, almost stepping into it in his blind self-absorption.

"And of what did Marcos speak?" Matthew finally asked.

The old men shook their heads. The oldest pointed to his own head as he shook it, in the universal language.

"Padre Marcos spoke of what they know not what," Felipe translated, "It was all very *estúpido* and they understood not a word of it. They carefully observed that only the very stupidest, the most vain, the worst lying tongues in the village relished it. This was very, very long ago. They left before it was over and never went back for another one. Nor would they ever speak to anyone of such things. The *santos* refused to listen to it and in the end, very few spoke to them at all. Before it happened. Now few speak to them for another reason, but they do listen to these old men at last."

"Listen to me," Matthew said directly to the two old men in the plain Kekchi that he was capable of, "You are very good fellows and Jesus loves you very much. Pray for me often, please, after I leave tonight. And pray to Our Lady often to keep you cautious and wise and close to the heart of Her Son."

Matthew quickly gave directions. "Bring Andre and Banto and Geraldo back to the village cemetery. Leave the third disciple of Marcos here, for now."

They all nodded seriously and slowly.

"Cover this ground carefully back to leave no sign. And—"

Matthew removed his pectoral cross, held it out before them.

"Now each of you swear you will never speak to anyone of this grave or this location. Nor of the disciple remaining here for now. Nor of anything we have spoken of today. All understood?"

"Si," they said in unison. They were actually very grateful.

"Now hold this cross and promise it to Jesus, and seal your promise by kissing the foot of His cross."

They all did so, with great reverence.

Casaroja

Father Matthew watched as they rolled up his poor priest and the two others in a tarp. Andre, what did you get into here? The leader or the led? I have no idea. And where on God's earth is this Marcos?

The men recovered the ground carefully, as instructed. They moved very quickly and everything would be fine, the priest saw. Matthew and Felipe found themselves nodding to each other. Still on target, my *companéro*.

Matthew stood there as the third disciple disappeared back under the dirt. He sprinkled some holy water on as they worked, prayed. But the full rites will have to await you, whoever you are. *Whatever you were.* A catechist, it seemed...if so, of *exactly what?* You are doubtful, very, very doubtful. Riddled with questions, even in death. And you will raise questions for which I have no answers, much less implications. You are nothing but trouble, Mystery Man. Everything about you is in question. Except for the fact that, even in death, you still are not safe for us to handle.

REQUIEM

Twilight slowly descended over the plaza of Casaroja, dozens of small candles glowing against it. The sky was clear and calm, hordes of birds passing over, their cries competing with those of the still mourning women. Many stood silently around the *cementerio* too, in groups of three or four. The final count was 67, including the unknown man up on the hill, but Matthew would mark it down officially for Salazar at 66.

Matthew stood at graveside with the others, before the straightened remains of Father Andre Meinrad Mondragon. A candle glowed either side of his skull. Matthew had first thought to keep his medals, but had finally given them back and carefully drawn them around his neck with fresh string. They were Andre's; he had carried them to the end. Doubtless he had finally come to know something profound about his Benedictine patron saint, even while still in this dimension. Father Andre's grave was the last one, at the foot of all those who, whatever else they had been, had ultimately and irrevocably become his people.

Father Matthew finished his prayers, made the sign of the cross. He had prayed solemnly and carefully, as a good superior should, he knew. But ah, angels seemed to mock him, do you not even have one little tear, to send your charge on his way? No, my *compadre*, what I said to Salazar was no lie. So long, Gabby, I never knew you.

Felipe had helped him erect a temporary altar, exactly over the place of the altar in Old San Tomás church. Some old crates and boxes were stacked up, but with beautiful Mayan embroidery draped over them. The candles were lit and a giant, silent crowd appeared. Felipe had said he could serve but did not know all the prayers. Fine, Matthew said, just do what you always do and watch my directions, I will read your part. He had also designated the two old Kekchi *santos*, father and son, sub-servers, and given them cards to lead all in some prayers in their language. It was a gesture that was not missed, nor was it meant to be.

His alb on, fixed with the cincture, Father Matthew slowly put on the maniple and stole, audibly whispering his prayers so those nearby could hear. He reached for his white chasuble.... No, he thought, not tonight. There was a full black chasuble he had also rolled up in his pack, for the old missionary option. It had been a long while since he had performed a Latin Mass; he was not even sure how well he recalled it. But everything he had seen pointed to the necessity of exercising the option, here and now. Father Augustine had been given it by the bishop of Cañada, years ago. In their foundings and journeys, Augustine and Matthew had often come upon remnants of ancient Catholic communities, old people who remembered nothing else. While the *indígena* had been baptized for centuries, missionary efforts were sporadic and often very rudimentary; you found yourself harking back to very tenuous roots, over and over. The liturgical changes of the 1960s had been only yesterday, and yesterday is what had been obliterated here. "So use the old Latin rites," Bishop Mara had insisted, "you and your priestly sons. Work up from the foundations as you may find them, and use what the oldest ones remember as occasions arise. Upon my authority, whenever you deem it fit."

I deem it fit today, Matthew judged, carefully refolding his white vestment. And I am the last of Augustine's priestly sons. And we are certainly going back to foundation level here tonight, dear God, if not beneath it, and trying to raise Your holy name up in this place once more. This is in truth a second start. And if the foundation is all that is left here, as with these ruined buildings, yet that true foundation had held—María and these two old men. Their earliest memories were of the Tridentine. Others might be less familiar with it, but afterwards would naturally ask María and the old men about it. *Our* key people, Matthew considered, yes; no one else could answer such questions. Certainly not any of the confused, presumptuous remnant of whatever may still be about, as a result of Andre's apparent catechetical misadventures.

Moreover, he involuntarily shuddered as he finished robing himself, the modernity of the white had seemed just plainly inappropriate at this moment, for this occasion. It was pure gut instinct; he could not really articulate why. Maybe it was my dream of the old Cologne altar, back on the Hill in my youth. Or maybe it was the cool night breeze arising beyond the trees, hitting the sweat still on the back of the neck, the priest mused, just the bracing effect. Yes, I would like to think that, but the truth is it had almost hit like a wall of repugnance, thinking of whiteness and the grinning teeth, especially in that last mysterious grave. Well, save *that* one for later, he figured. And save the white vestment for another day, too, when we might finally have enough distance for a "celebration of the lives of these dead." But there are going to be no camp fire songs, this evening. There has not even been a proper mourning, much less the awestruck prayer of the old Requiem.

Or maybe it was just the color of those Adidas shoes....

A solemn Felipe appeared along with Toda, as they had been instructed. In the dying light Father Matthew saw that the *indígena*'s face was as old as he had ever seen it, as old as this land. Someone had given him a stole to wear for his task of acolyte, immaculately white and with images of Our Lady of Guadalupe on either side. Only God knew where they had secreted it during the terrors, how it had been so well preserved until tonight.

They lined up in procession and the candle-carrying women were already singing. Matthew led them all up to the great square grave site, the boys with the sticks and the blankets still keeping patrol on the looming scavenger birds. The candles were arranged all at one side like a table of vigil lights upon his instructions, and removed from the graves.

"Come to their assistance, you saints of God...." Matthew prayed. And slowly, reverently walked around the entire area, sprinkling the dead with holy water. They were all virtually covered in a thick bed of flowers, only a few pieces of skull or bone picking up the reflected light.

Casaroja

"Receive their souls and offer them in the sight of the Most High."

He nodded to Felipe: go to it. Ringing the bells Felipe led the procession back into the area of the destroyed church, followed by Toda and the two old *santos* with little candles, followed by Father Matthew who went up toward the altar, and kissed it. He signaled his servers to kneel, bowed solemnly, and made the sign of the cross.

"Introibo ad altare Dei. Ad Deum qui laetificat juventutem meam. Judica me Deus, et discerne causum meam de geste non sancta: ab homine iniquo et doloso erue me...."

Father Matthew, kneeling with Felipe and Toda at either side, began the Requiem Mass, a perfect line of the Maya in their resplendent best just behind them, all carrying lighted candles and reverently bowed toward the altar.

Afterwards, Matthew would be able to remember virtually none of it. It was as if he had entered a trance carrying him back to the very old days he had been a server himself, at Requiem Masses with the old priests at his hometown parish before he even had gone down to Saint Benedict's. But it was not a trance, he recalled, it was eternal time: the Latin, the pace, the rubrics hit him like a cold bracing wind, fierce but cleansing and invigorating. Dear suffering Savior, the old rite of Your sacrifice can scour anything clean, even this. To his amazement, Matthew had even felt his entire rage and anger go up and dissolve in that furious bath; he would not have thought it possible. And not only his rage at what had happened here at Casaroja, not even at what had occurred in this whole country these several years. It went very far back, had indeed been something in himself, something indefinable but there for decades, something you were so used to you did not even think about it anymore.

But the priest also saw that the black Requiem was having the same effect on these people gathered here. Scouring them, cutting deep as a hurricane. You could not even believe this miracle was happening, but it was. You saw the azure sky go violet, the red sunset vanish, that mass of stars quickly blink on...you saw pieces of faces in the candle light, heard the bells.... There was the virtually shocked face of Felipe, the inscrutability of Toda, the leathery calm of the old father and son, not shocked at all. You saw the gibbous moon rise and climb in the night sky. There too was the catlike presence, felt only now, of the second, silent María. And María Bon's own green, almost prophetic eyes gazing, penetrating this space.

Yes, you could certainly believe it. For in this rite you were unequivocally praying *for* the dead, not *to* them as if they were already among the blessed. And the people had needed to do that, the last thing for their loved ones—to give, rather than receive. "The ladder welding heaven to earth..." he remembered Father Ambrose's lesson all the way back from minor seminary. And felt a cool breeze continuing across the plaza, as if merged with his dream-memory of Mass with Augustine and Christopher at the old altar at Saint Benedict's. For good Jesus' sake, these *indígena* themselves, the past two days, have had enough peasant sense not only to pray for their dead, but to argue with them. Thankfully, the two Catholic priests here in the days leading up to chaos had failed to fully effectuate the divorce between eternity and the here and now.

After the readings which Matthew gave both in Latin and in Kekchi, there had been little point whatsoever in a sermon. He had been going to say something, again, as he had said to the couples: we will be back. He had been going to say something about these dead. But this invisible gale blew it all away, as if through the vanished roof and vanished walls of San Tomás church. Dear Lord, it is all gone already. What can I tell them of their own horrors, their own loved ones? And what more can one say of whatever impossible idiocy had entered here?

No, Matthew had considered, I have just encountered it myself, I am still in shock myself in the shadow of this lunatic beast that has set murderous suspicion between all, even amidst families, and between these people and their own priest. And I do not even know the answers yet myself. The murderers were soldiers, yes. It was a sort of genocide, certainly. But he remembered an old lesson from his friend Christopher—a lawyer, of all things. That oath you give witnesses really does mean something, Christopher had said once, "The truth, the whole truth, and nothing but the truth." So what good was an incomplete truth? And what good was any statement from the man who sent Andre Meinrad Mondragon, and God knows who else in his wake, and all those words, words, words with them.

Casaroja

Nothing but the truth? Who could even say? You? And anyway, those two old men had said it all: *it was all very estúpido and they understood not a word of it.*

Time to shut up, finally, the priest soberly determined. Time to be Catholic, for once, however late. Let Christ's own gift to His apostles speak, nothing else: "Do this in remembrance of Me." Cut out all the talk, finally, just say the Mass and pray. So in place of any homily, he just, quite consciously, sat down on the red vinyl chair at that part of the service. He bowed his head, placed his hands on his knees in silence and repentance. And then finally signaled those two old *santos*, to lead the people in standard prayers for the dead in Kekchi, a bit of a restart on the catechesis. These two men, silent for years at the heart of this turbulence: *let both their faithfulness in sound prayer and pious silence speak now, Lord Jesus, at last, and let this sign visibly and indelibly reroute the minds and spirits of these people: it is from here we must start over again.*

So he rode that out, happy to disappear, disappearing wholly even from his own consciousness into the mystery of Consecration. Starting to come out of it, a little, at Communion, he saw all the faces he would doubtless remember some unexpected day or night but upon whom now he could not even focus; take this Body…take this Body….

And finally led them all back, the final time, to their dead. They were all singing, high and unearthly, and some had brought out instruments too—deep low drums and *chirimia*. The night held all together and the space around the gravesite glowed.

"Dies irae, dies illa," Matthew remembered his own voice intoning, as if it belonged to someone else, as he began his long circuit of the dead. "Solvet saeclum in favilla, Teste David cum Sibylla…."

The heads of every person in the village of Casaroja, restored to the best semblance of sacred order and time that Matthew could achieve, were all deeply bowed.

"Libera me, Domine, de morta aeterna, in die illa tremenda: Quando coeli movendi sunt et terra: Dum veneris judicare saeculum per ignum…."

DEPARTINGS

As he packed up his saddlebags Father Matthew could still hear them singing across the plaza. They would probably be singing all night into the morning. A great red glow over it all could be seen, as they filled in the mass grave under torch lights. He had allowed them finally to keep the incense censor, these Kekchi Mayans loved incense so well. The clouds went up and held the reflected light from the flames in suspension over all, in this enclosed space within the dense, deeply darkened forest.

He had finally become reflective, now that his work here, at least for now, was finished. For one thing, cruel as the thought was, his own personal career facilitator old Jack Wildenmut was going to ask all about this sooner or later, probably sooner, and want a report. Heck, he'll probably want something for *The American Benedictine Review*, Matthew figured. Yet Matthew was going back in memory in a direction quite different. To those very early days in the minor seminary with Christopher, listening in rapt attention as old Father Ambrose Houck lectured on Benedictine history. How amazing it would have been to have known Saint Benedict Archabbey's great founder from Switzerland, Abbot—later Bishop—Henry Henni, who built his life upon the conviction that living and working among the Indian peoples was the only certain way to their conversion, to lead by direct example of their order's way of prayer and work. Father Ambrose had the fond habit of reading Abbot Henni's letters straight out of the Saint Benedict archives. The old missionary's teaching that such conversion, by example, was the original charism of the Order of Saint Benedict, had burned an indelible stamp upon Father Matthew Eberhard's subsequent career as priest and missionary.

In his rucksack journals as he labored across the raw Dakota plains in the 1870s, Abbot Henni was never too occupied to scrawl more upon the subject, no matter his crushing labors or the inclement weather. Some of Matthew's favorite passages had found their way into his own thesis, the only really decent parts of that sorry enterprise, Matthew had come to think. Did you read those too, Andre, he mused, did these reflections of our very own Father Abraham mean anything, in the whole wide world, to you? One passage he could practically quote, "It is God's will that the Order of Saint Benedict in our days resume missionary work among the world's heathens." This was the Benedictine task in all times, Henni argued—conversion and civilization—and if they had stayed at it there would not have been, in his lifetime, 500 million children "in darkness and the shadow of death."

Death, Andre, the prior thought, as he buckled up his saddlebags for a long journey, and not the sort of death unleashed here, either. Death in the very oldest Catholic sense, as in Saint John's Gospel and the Didache: death of the soul as opposed to the road of life. For there are only two ways, dear Father Andre...but did anyone ever actually teach you that? It is only these simplest and plainest things we find so hard, anymore.

Andre, if he had truly been as smart as all the *periti* had certified he was, may have at some level feared he would never find one to properly guide him. His prior was beginning to dimly perceive this. While forever silent, the objective evidence concerning the missionary priest, Andre Meinrad Mondragon, was that zeal and counsel on the level of Abbot Henry Henni was wholly unknown to him. He had not even turned to myself or Augustine, either. Of course Andre gave that final, terribly unforgettable outward impression of having been quite cocksure. But the evidence of the graves was that his public face was only the most pathetic of masks for deep confusion, utter rootlessness. For so quickly he had turned to that cipher Marcos.

As for Marcos, if he were as cunning as this crime scene indicated, he would have feared only that time was running out, that it already was no longer safe here. So, between the two of them, one was more wise than the other. Wise as a hawk, and as cruel.

And that was the scenario if Marcos was on *our* side, Prior Matthew brooded....

So unwind your own riddle, Padre, Matthew finally instructed himself at last. The time here had been compressed, flew by cruelly—Andre here barely a year. The Kekchi had lived through years of this civil war, during which however the mission's own were rarely touched. But after Andre's brief tenure as shepherd here, 67 dead including two who had come very far from home. You wanted in your imagination to see Andre's priestly arm, though now buried, still flung high over all the others, still blessing them. But what you had instead was a scornful reflection of your own naiveté, mixed with some yet unfathomable lie at this mocking sea's floor. Neither a practical nor even a mystic tie to any genuine Benedictine vision of what ought to have been, whatsoever. No, unwind it you cannot. Not your program, hardly Abbot Henni's. Nor even your own riddle—only Marcos'. Or whoever's....

All this, of course, only led to the deeper riddle—the one already making Father Matthew's blood boil: how Andre and Marcos had come together, the old chicken or the egg question. For who exactly had betrayed the mission, Matthew brooded, and inferentially, also betrayed me? Andre, *solus?* From day one? Good old Columban "Jack" Wildenmut? Or was Marcos just a con artist come revolutionary at large? It was all so scrambled that, for purposes of analysis, you had to think of all of them as one: not just a Father Andre, nor a Father Marcos, nor an Archbishop Wildenmut. Rather all of them together, and all far off Abbot Henni's charts, sharing at the very least a whole new and rather fictive Father Abraham. And nothing like Abbot Henni, either. No. A whole new Father Abraham, certainly, with a whole new program, intent on taking everything back to Genesis, as it were, to some sort of idealized Eden out of a sophomoric game plan, forging a New Frontier in this multifaceted wilderness, otherwise known as the parish of San Tomás, Casaroja.

How am I, as prior, even going to fix something like this? Matthew wondered. For it had nothing at least fundamentally to do with Guatemala, either, Matthew was coming to dimly see, for

Casaroja

once. Nor for that matter, really at center, did it pivot precisely on the struggle between Communism versus the free world—although both, sure, were competing here. At true center, however, there was an eerie, cavalier similarity to those two behemoths, as the Skeed had aptly called them: a cold indifference to how their footprints might crush genuine communities, individual lives. The Skeed was on to this paradox himself, however absurdly the insight failed to deter him from continuing to drink his Marxism straight. Where on earth could you hatch a fellow that shallow? Well, Matthew turned the thought over, I do not really need to ask…I just stood in a trench which smelled deeply of something seriously askew out of my own country. Something rather different than the high-flown talk about democracy and liberty you heard traveling south from home. The fact is, Matthew had to admit, I have hardly been in the USA for years; even a crackerjack like the Skeed is better tuned in.

Yeah, score one for you, little Father Skeed. Or half a score, anyway. In a realm where you and I really have neither the background nor much serious business, Stevie boy, unless you count our surfeit of opinions on all subjects, good Yankees we. I at least tried to stay out of this *liberación* folly, Matthew knew. But it had already gone too far and grown too big for this little mission station's good. Right under my nose, of course…. So upon a half-truth they go marching, these hapless Central American surrogates of the land of the free and the home of the brave. Reflecting both of our patented home teams too, and manifesting on either side of the local political fence. Then simply dumped into this bloody sandbox of garbled words and ideas, ever evolving. Until death do them part. For we have to go far offshore anymore, with appropriate stand-ins, to play out that lethal brand of sport no longer allowed on home turf, where not even dog fighting is legal anymore. But we can still place blood sport bets on *this* ground, where sequential incarnations of our passing idols—now "left," now "right," but always insistently materialist—duel in the sun.

In a way, Matthew rued, we Benedictines had already been on board for thirty years before the fall out. On board with the old idea of development, above and beyond helping to provide the basic things, food and medicine, shelter and rudimentary education. It was his own old debate, too, with the mission's founder, his own mentor

Father Augustine, of course. Augustine, bless him, who recalled the good old days with his International Scout full of relief supplies underwritten by Senator Karl Mundt. But becoming conduits for government grants and old-style social uplift had rather set us up for something of a back seat role, Matthew felt. Especially when government, politics, and economics changed, and the Big Pictures in those departments concocted by our own fellow American citizens changed, as shaped by their new leaders. It would certainly be worse, of course, if godless Marxism were triumphant here.... Sure, you always had to remember that. Yet if conversion was reduced to no more than upgrading the standard of living, or the sophistication of entertainment, would the defeat of either the new *cacique* in Guatemala City, or for that matter, of *la revolución*, justify our order spending a single day more here?

Who, then, was this season's new Father Abraham? That I, in my unwitting negligence, apparently opened the gate to.... Well, we already had a few clues, in the manner of Sherlock Holmes. Or perhaps, Matthew grimly thought, a few examples of "praxis" in action.... A likely proponent of liberation "from existing structures" wearing trendy running shoes. A too-well known cultural anthropologist sporting a modish Saint Benedict medal. One quite mysterious state of the art *wunderkind* from central casting, who split to fight another day. And two local water carriers who also went down with the ship.

Was there somewhere though a vague, distant hand in this catastrophe, which neither split at the last possible moment nor stayed, but imagined itself the One Great Shaping Hand? From the current *americáno* administration, or a holdover from the last? What difference did it make, and who cared anyway? Last season's champs, with whom our perpetually tardy churchmen were ecstatic to join, were last seen manning antiwar barricades in our own streets, painting government buildings with animal blood. Our proud nation's new guys, on the other hand, showed up dressed for success, and chomping cigars like small town bankers. And my mistake, the prior knew, was just to laugh them all off; he had never taken the dueling Father Abrahams of his nation very seriously. He wondered: should I rethink that now? But how even to navigate amidst such strategies?

Casaroja

So am I missing something here, Matthew still relentlessly wondered? I, the late-blooming seminary student complete with celebrated thesis—itself with no shortage of pre-packaged rhetoric to please teacher? For again, what did the counterfeit options of either Marxist utopia or "unlimited consumer choice" really have to do with the Kingdom of Jesus Christ? Could you try to merge such paleface fantasies with large slabs of something like Teilhard de Chardin, maybe, turn anthro-babble into mystic tie babble, and light out toward the Omega Point? I never looked that far ahead, Prior Matthew Eberhard had to admit, despite pockets stuffed with iceberg warnings. All I ever knew was the gibberish. It was enough for my teacher, Jack loved it too, and I was launched. Good luck, anyway, *compadres*. Or perhaps, based on the admittedly partial returns available here, truly bad luck.

I wonder if there is somewhere to safely field test this brew, he sheepishly wondered, like Kentucky whiskey.... Apparently you could carry this sort of thing off only so long as the pre-packaged Liberation did not become tangible enough to provoke an army to exterminate it. If this crushing reality *still* did not unwind the riddle, there nonetheless was one true, certified praxis for you, boys, anyway: stay at least three steps removed. Ah, poor Andre, you finally were not even very good at praxis, either.

But then too, Andre, Matthew had to shake his head to himself, I already sense that you will become legendary in time. Already in life you had become symbolic. Legendary as your own saint and namesake, perhaps, at least within our order. And disturbingly symbolic as that cock-eyed attempt to run Saint Benedict's medal through the grinding wheel of modern art. It had all seemed rather harmless, until today. A shadow of the basic design was still there, of course, the saint's face on the front and a cross on the back. But again, there was no room in such a stylish sweep of stuck-in-the-1960s aestheticism for words to ward off Satan. Unlucky you were there, my friend and brother. And in a giving a wink to that trendy Catholic milieu which was relegating such protection to the closet, you speedily became a hostage of luck and blind chance. You were going to turn unlucky sooner or later.

Matthew threw his saddlebags over his shoulder, picked up his well-rolled and packed blanket, and made his way over toward his horse.

"Deliver him, oh Lord, from eternal death," Matthew prayed the absolution prayers over again to himself, "and for that matter, deliver me. From that dreadful day when the heavens and earth shall be moved, and when old words find entirely new—and absolutely berserk—meanings. When day is night and utopia a world of slaughter. When we boldly call Your own way of life, death, and try to auto-generate true death into our own fondest, most false substitute for Your Life. When You come to judge the world by fire...."

Matthew shook his head. All these catechists too—such as these two local dead with Andre—were one thing. But what about their actual *content*, these catechetical programs? Doubtless, whatever mysteries remain, in the little remnant of an ecclesiastical structure you could discern here—Marcos, Andre and the dead buried with him—you could already sense a not unfamiliar pattern. "The new ecclesiology" they called it, or the "base community." Take a six week's trial run, and if not completely delighted return to sender for a total refund.

And how many of these program guides have you even read *yourself*, Father Prior, before you sent Mr. Whoever out with them? Did you even take the time to sift through them, figure out what precisely any of it had to do with the salvation of the soul, and what merely with getting on board with the current fashions of the *periti*? And further, whatever choice variations of this fare had been devised, for the hyper-initiated Andre to get himself mixed up with out here, at the end of that literally patented and copyrighted flat world, how fundamentally different was that from what we *all* routinely do? Forgetting that the Mystical Body only grows one soul at a time, as Abbot Henni taught. By grace, by genuine conversion.

For how could you focus on mere methodology, our Dearly Beloved Praxis, rather than upon the substance and object of the conversion experience: the individual soul, as divinely created? Specially. Uniquely. To be approached, finally, in its intimacy, only as Christ approached anyone He met. Not by something purchased and shipped in a box. Dear God in heaven, does somebody out there really believe that such a thing, complete with brochures and 60-day discounts for bulk purchases, constitutes a challenge to "existing, dominant structures"?

But dear Lord, no, no, I did not want to read them. I did not even know what was in whatever box that I allowed Andre to carry out here. Except that, sure, it was something his handlers liked. Well—get over *that* one, Padre. Say it: *my* handlers. My very own boosters and "facilitators," as the jargon goes....

And meditating along those lines, here came Toda now, followed by Felipe with that maddeningly accusatory countenance: the dead man's face and birdlike beak. But then, under the weight of terrible self-accusation, Matthew remembered: of course. How easy yourself to forget. And how many times have I tried to look away? But a true priest can never look away. No excuses there, either, for thinking that your work today was done. For one thing is left to do, one very important thing.... Good Felipe....

* * *

The horse's head leaned forward, turning. It took a couple more steps forward and stopped, as if it were nodding, the big eyes blinking and nose flaring. He can smell the trail, Father Matthew figured, rubbing the horse's neck. He turned to see Felipe and Toda coming up behind on the burros, also packed to leave. Beyond them was the red glow of torch lights from the plaza, the silhouettes of the cross and the remaining fragment of wall against it. The men were filling in the mass grave; you could hear the rustle of dirt and shovels.

"This is your money piece, horse," Matthew said low into the animal's ear. He had reverted to talking to it generically, more comfortable with that, "Are you excited? I'll bet you are."

He looked at his watch: after eleven already. They would go up the road to where it split, as they had discussed, and then Matthew would run as far as he could in the cover of the night, past as many of the local habitations as he could. The horse might well run very well, without having to walk behind the burros. He remembered the condition of that trail as being pretty good. At least he should be able to maintain a healthy trot. The women had graciously brought him some food and baked goods, and been delighted when he had asked for extra, as rewards for the animal.

"It's time to do your bit for God and country," Matthew kept talking lowly to the horse. It seemed to like that last one; one might even say it was smiling. "Do it for the monkey house and all that. If you do real good and I make it to paradise, there will be a picture of you in my mind's eye forever, courtesy of God who preserves all things beautiful, and in that way you will be immortalized. Wouldn't you like that? Sebastian, the Hero Horse of Casaroja. That could be you."

It was difficult to say if the horse liked that precisely, but it was perceptively obvious that the beast responded well to the sound of its own name. It rubbed its lips against Matthew's shirt and nodded happily.

"Yes, Sebastian," Matthew tried to say, gamely as he could. "And if we make it back to San Plácido I'll even throw a feast day for you, throw in a nice bath and scrub down, too. I'll bet you would like that, wouldn't you, Sebastian?"

The horse nodded vigorously at that, straining at the bit. He was ready, all right. The priest patted him hard on his neck. "Whoa, boy, just a minute, now. Then you do your stuff. Do it well and you will be a legend."

The women had returned to send him off, the same group from the beginning with Juano. The boy looked somewhat firmer and straighter than before. And the women, despite their grieving, were much more comfortable with him than at the beginning. It was strange.

"We'll be back, soon," he said to María Bon, firmly, trying to keep down the emotion, "I...."

I what? Who do you think you are, Padre, MacArthur? Don't make any promises you cannot keep, especially now.

"I'll see to that. If I can't come back myself, I'll send you the best I have. As soon as it's safe for all of us, understand? This new government is still shaky and is still trying to figure out what happened. It is not totally in control yet, either, everywhere as it should be."

"Yes, certainly, Padre Matthew." The little woman's bright, strong eyes glowed even in this dark. It felt rotten not to be able to give her any better but that was all there was.

"Hopefully a year at the longest, six months if I can. There are even now still some troubles, especially to the west. Soldiers are still at large, and some civil patrols. There are good people working to make things stable, though. It might change soon, they are working on it." He turned to Felipe, "Please have Toda translate what I just said as precisely as he can, Felipe, so all these women understand. This is very important."

"Sí, Padre."

Toda did so and he could see all the women nodding, touching their hands to their hearts in their way.

"Now María Bon," he leaned over, "please say your rosaries for me because your prayers are more important than you know. And now tell me, please, one thing…."

There was virtually no time for this, he knew. But with all the activity and the earlier reticence, some quite humanly understandable—my God, this woman had seen two sons unearthed and reburied—he had not gotten to the core subject with her, their old "key person" in this village. Despite what he had already seen and been able to discern from fragmentary pieces, her testimony was doubtless the most essential. If only there were more time….

He enunciated his Spanish very slowly, looking her clearly in the eyes, "María, *por favor*, tell me about Marcos."

Matthew could see that, while emotional, her response was detailed and substantive. Toda translated when she injected idioms in Kekchi, and then Felipe repeated all of it:

"He was a very hard man, I think, Padre, I cannot say. I had little to do with him after the first two months. He started much trouble among the people, but the truth is long before the end we all got wise to him, him and his *compadres*. Banto and Geraldo were only *idiota*. Marcos trained them to lead the talks. But after Marcos stopped coming as often, no one went to listen to just those two. They spoke of our Blessed Savior and His Mother as if they were two stupid peasants. I am sorry I held back till now; I thought they all were with you."

"Please, María, be sorry for nothing. And always be that wise."

"Bueno, Padre."

"Now tell me about the other disciple of Marcos. The one who wore white shoes."

"Ah!" The woman suddenly exclaimed. "So they killed him too!" It was not a question of any kind, just a statement. She had obviously deduced it, but his two *santos* and the grave diggers had clearly been good to their word and not circulated anything about it.

"I of course can say nothing about him to anyone, María. Nor should you to anyone else."

"I understand. Thank you for your understanding. However, allow me to say this of Carlo, *no one alive knows anything*." Toda repeated that to Felipe, who in turn translated it very precisely to the priest. "He was for certain men only," she concluded, "and those men were all killed."

"Carlo was his name?"

"Sí."

"The old man said he was neither Kekchi nor a *ladino* of this country."

"I think I agree. I only know his name from Padre Marcos, who brought him and left him here."

"*Left* him here?"

"Sí, *Padre*. When the others would journey away, at times."

"Which others journey away?"

"All of them—Marcos, Padre Andre, even Banto and Geraldo. Carlo never left...."

"Why?"

"This to me is unknown, Padre. I had nothing to do with any of that or their business. Who can even say anything about such fellows? Who can even know if those were really their names?"

"My only man was Padre Andre Mondragon."

"I understand that now."

"But I want you with complete honesty to tell me about Andre and Marcos."

"He brought Marcos. Not long after he came here. Then Marcos started the little groups and meetings."

"And what would Padre Andre do at those meetings?"

"Sit and listen." She said it firmly and directly as possible.

Casaroja

Matthew found himself half-turning away from this sound woman, in shame. He already really knew it, of course, but it was shameful to hear it. "What else particularly bothered you?" he managed to continue.

"That Marcos then would come time to time, and say Mass only in the red house, not in San Tomás."

"In the red house and *not* in San Tomás?"

"Sí."

"Why?"

The recurrent question seemed again to befuddle her. She was shaking her head, gravely. There was no time for it anyway. He looked back at Felipe and Toda. They nodded; they were loaded and ready.

Then María began to speak, evenly. "I understand that Marcos was of a group of men of which the soldiers were highly interested," she said, "When people told the soldiers he was gone they were not believed." She had said it all drolly and matter of factly at last, as the considered answer to the last question. She was no longer befuddled, but apparently she had to use a degree of willpower to admit it, even to herself. Matthew nodded; he had dimly begun to assume that, and also to resist it and all its implications, but here was the confirmation.

Suddenly the woman was speaking again, very full of emotion, her little voice ringing clear as a bell in the night, her small, sculpted face animated and her eyes alive. "Padre Matthew, your man was not a man but a boy." She stated it with crisp definiteness.

"Sí," Matthew said, with great respect.

"He was *el subordinado de Marcos*. The *patán* of Marcos!!" She bit the word off so harshly the spit went flying. The word had a very exact meaning: the worst sort of clown, a country bumpkin, even to other rustics.

"Did it have anything to do with all this?" Matthew waved his arm out to encompass the whole plaza, the entire tragedy.

"Perhaps something, only God knows. Marcos disappeared just two days before the soldiers came."

"*Two days?*"

"Sí, sí, Padre Matthew. Then the day after Padre Marcos left there was heard to be a little warfare nearby. It was also spoken of.

And the day after that the soldiers came. But many think it would have happened anyway...."

"I...perhaps...yes, that may well be true," Matthew said, only as not to upset her. Nobody had so clearly spoken of this, up to now, either, the priest shook his head to himself. And sure, I could speculate, but why sow useless confusion with her? It was all too much and he was far from drawing conclusions, especially on this new testimony. It was time to go.

"Those men who destroyed us were monsters," María was shaking her fist, "Is there no justice?"

"María, in this world, sometimes. I pray for that. But not always, no."

"You are an honest *padre*."

"I wish you were my sister," Matthew said, and meant it. He reached over to mark the cross on her forehead, then blessed them all.

The animals were already moving.

"Good-bye, María Bon."

She and the others watched the animals enter the forest path, disappear enveloped in darkness.

"You are my brother through Jesus Christ and His Mother Mary in heaven!" her voice rang out after him at last, against that wall of night, triumphantly.

GIFTS

For a long time Felipe stood at the crossroads, watching in the direction Padre Matthew had disappeared up the narrow forest path back to the mountains. He had heard the horse walk off, then after some distance the sound of the priest's voice, commanding the animal, and finally fading hoof beats against the dirt.

He was still full of amazement, in a state approaching shock. Less than a week before he had stood dripping with sweat near a waterfall, the cool handle of a deadly knife in his grip. The memory of it still burned him like a hot brand, making him flinch and instinctively dig his fingernails into his palm, as if scratching it would make it go away. He could almost scream out in pain! And where was my mind, good Lord? Full of insanity—I was coiled and about to spring like a panther—murder Your holy priest! Oh Madre María! The inside of my mind throbbing with visions of the thigh, aiming for it, hungry to tear open a great hole and let him die! Seeing it in my head over and over like a movie! It is as if the very recall of those thoughts press against the inside of my skull and make it want to explode. My own hard determination, my blindness! And to have come within seconds of being a killer myself. Like the monsters who had come here—no different! And all this mere days ago!

But then too, every inch of his flesh sang out in thankfulness, for that split second of holy hesitation that had caused him to wait, opened up his natural senses to observe what was actually happening. And that split second had somehow, he would never understand how, been instantaneously invaded by grace, a free gift of God. A free gift! And continued opening into confession, into further prayers, the scales falling from the eyes, relief! And finally flowing out like a river into the numbing encounter with mass murder here, and that same priest's careful dispensing of grace and order.

And now he was gone, that good priest! What will I do, Madre María? I must pray very, very hard....

Just twenty minutes ago, Padre Matthew had stopped, taken Felipe aside, and given him his final instructions. "Beware Felipe, I tell you again, of that 'brotherhood.' I fear for your downfall! You have an open and very generous nature, young man. You have many astonishing gifts. Do you realize what you have just accomplished here, in just two days, aiding me and these people? You must never forget it the rest of your life! You must always remember that this was the day your true life began!"

Reassuringly, Padre Matthew had set out a schedule for their future encounter. After a few months that the priest said he needed to attend to other business, he would expect Felipe at the priory where he should be prepared to stay at least three full days They would discuss catechism and the things he needed to know about the true Christian life. In the meantime, Felipe should tell the woman Inés what he was doing. They needed to consider marriage, come to a conclusion about it and end the affair the way it had gone. If she wanted to embark on marriage, the priest would see her on another occasion. "We cannot go beyond that now," Padre Matthew had cautioned, "the true God has given each of us free will, which properly is the will to love and serve Him. But neither you nor I can make that decision for her. Acceptance to marriage must be freely given." And the priest also made him understand his own obligations continued, no matter what, to this woman and their child.

Overwhelmed, spinning with the reality of choices and consequences, Felipe could not even think. Such grace for me... amidst all these dead! His mind could not even focus on such a mystery; his face could not free itself of the flow of tears. He only relished the sound of this new friend's voice, his holy counsel, hard

Casaroja

as it was. The whole façade of the false friendships fell away like so much fog. And just behind them, maddeningly spinning illusions made up of violent, insane movies, monstrous music, deranged scripts. Anyone would have said I was crazed, he realized. My soul was soaked through with mesmerizing confections styled by turbulent and befouled strangers, I was charged with visions and passions which did not even emanate from within myself. No wonder I was so blind, no wonder I could be so easily possessed by this murderous spirit that is devouring our country! Anything, anything Lord but that, again! That ridiculous brotherhood of the *cantina* friends, crazy Pedro and the rest of the *compañeros*. No more! And those intoxicating fantasies of cinema mayhem—dear, dear God! What did I think violence was, death was? Or what I was, myself?

He turned to Toda; the *indígena* looked sad too, head bowed. He understood Felipe fully, nodded silently. It was time they got on.

Night birds squawked in the forest, deep within. The thick air itself stung and his clothes were still caked with graveyard mud and his own salty sweat. Funny, Felipe thought, for all of my fantasies of heroism, of adventure and daring, sex and greed, it was as if I had become totally out of my body. With that thought he shivered; he still hardly knew why. For actually, the night was sultry warm. His sweaty body scratched and ached; insects were biting him and were flying into his face. Yet for all that physical discomfort, it spoke of being in the flesh, in God's world, the way He wanted you to be at this moment. Here and now, in a world which was. The alternative.... He shivered again, as if hit by a lash.

"Ah Lord," he prayed within himself now, "whatever it takes! I will never go back!" For he had learned a lesson too vast to fathom quickly: this salt was better than the vile sugars of his movie induced and alcohol induced fantasies.

And so he turned and followed Toda now, bowing in both amazed wonder and chastened obedience. Oh Lord, I had always longed for adventure, just like in the movies, but I would have never dreamed the actual one which, all along, You had planned for me....

He opened his eyes wide along the dark trail, let his night vision soak in. He gripped his bridle and rode on, trying to let the air penetrate his throbbing skull. And he prayed. Eventually his sweat evaporated; he felt the jungle's cool. Every sound and smell, every sight was a gift and a wonder. His body returned to his command, there only remaining the burden of his blasted memories, the sting of his still live grief.

Ὠ

A NOTE ON THE AUTHOR

Michael Morow was born in Hammond, Indiana in 1951. He is a 1977 graduate of Valparaiso University School of Law and has been engaged in the practice of law for 36 years. Besides his profession, he has been active as a lecturer in adult Catholic education and for home schools. A photographer, his lifetime archive is online as M Roy M at flickr.com. *The Long Exile*, a series of his novels focusing on contemporary American Catholics and their missionary endeavors, has been underway for over a decade and is now coming into print. The author is a lifelong student of American literature, monasticism, and Dante. He works in Indianapolis where he lives with his wife Jewell, an attorney and librarian who contributes research assistance and editorial advice to *The Long Exile* project.

A NOTE ON DESIGN

This book is set in a digitalized version of 17th century Janson font, created by the Hungarian Nicholas Kis (1650-1702), who was influenced by Dutch typemasters.

The mask on the cover was collected in the early 1960s in Alta Verapaz, Guatemala. It is the figure of a Spanish conquistador soldier, from the Dance of the Conquistadors, and is the type of mask worn by Father Andre Meinrad Mondragon in Father Matthew's dream sequence in the novel.